Nevada Jade

Linda Lee Chaikin

ACCENT BOOKS
Denver, Colorado

ACCENT BOOKS

A division of Accent Publications, Inc.
12100 West Sixth Avenue
P.O. Box 15337
Denver, Colorado 80215

Copyright © 1990 Accent Publications, Inc.
Printed in the United States of America

Library of Congress Catalog Card Number 89-82126

ISBN 0-89636-262-0

To Steve

My own frontier hero. . .who
happens to be my husband of 18
years. Thanks for being there
always.

Chapter 1

Strawberry Flat in the High Sierras
1860

"This miserable predicament is all your fault, Jade O'Neil," Holly gritted. She swayed from side to side as the Overland Stage tottered over the Sierra Nevada pass hedged with thick, gray-green pine. It was late afternoon on their first day out from Placerville, California on their way to Washoe, recently rechristened Virginia City.

Jade gripped the seat, her green eyes riveted out the window on the steep drop below where the American River tumbled across the whitish rocks. "Don't look—it will be all right soon," said Jade, surprised that her voice was calm.

Holly O'Neil bounced in her seat and struggled to keep from landing across the coach on her sister's lap.

"What's the matter with that driver?"

Holly leaned out the window. "Slow down, Mister! You want to get us all killed?"

"Yee-aay-ee!" The whip cracked above the heads of the horses. "Hang on, ladies. Ol' Harry will have ya at Berry's Flat in time for beef 'n beans!"

Jade moaned at the suggestion. Her long illness had left her with little appetite, and her stomach felt queasy.

"Beef 'n beans!" Holly moaned with a sniff. "Jade, are you sure Pa wrote telling us to come to Virginia City? How come I never saw the letter?"

Jade, listening intently to the wheels creaking as they struggled through the well-worn ruts, hoped to ignore the question. There had been no answer from Thomas O'Neil to her urgent letter informing him of their mother's death.

"We've no choice, Holly, and you know it. With the house sold for back taxes, we've no place to go but Virginia City. Don't worry so. Pa will be waiting for us at Strawberry Flat," she said with more confidence than she felt. "He's probably there now with a wagon."

"And if he isn't? By the time we reach the stopover it'll be evening. You saw the hordes of miners and gamblers at Placerville. They're all headed straight for Virginia City! Strawberry Flat will be packed with the smelly creatures." Holly wrinkled her pert nose. "Just what are we going to do? Eat and sleep in the same common room with gamblers and gunslingers?"

"Stop it, Holly. You'll frighten Shaun," but it was Jade who felt her muscles tighten. Suppose Thomas O'Neil was *not* there to meet them? She had been thinking about that very thing for the last few hours. Since the news of the silver find in the Comstock Lode, the rush to Washoe had been on. Men were everywhere, riding horses, mules, or walking with packs on their backs, all headed for one location—the great silver discovery on Sun Mountain.

At the mention of being frightened, Shaun O'Neil, a sensitive, handsome boy of eight, managed a brave smile. "I'm not scared, Jade," he offered, obviously trying to encourage his older sister. "Neither is Keeper."

The boy held tightly to the quivering black and white kitten hidden under his coat. The cat was obviously frightened in spite of his master's declaration, and Shaun kept a rope tied to its collar so it couldn't dart off. Jade understood how much the cat meant to him. The night before she had overheard him praying before going to bed, and the childish words still rang in her heart. *Please, Lord Jesus, take care of Keeper. . . . Mama's with you, and he's all I got left to hold tight. Help me be a man, help us find our Pa—but especially Uncle Samuel with the Indians. Amen.*

Jade sighed and looked out the window. As the stage twisted up the trail through the forest, a roughly hewn wood and canvas structure came into view. A weather-beaten sign read Berry's Flat. The stopover was far from being a welcome sight. It was owned by an inhospitable man named Berry, but the tavern offered food, a stable for the mules and horses, and a common sleeping room.

The stage rumbled to a halt and Jade stepped down, feeling a blast of bitter wind shake her ebony curls.

"Oooh—it's freezing!" gasped Holly. "Didn't I tell you this was the wrong time to come? The man in Placerville told us we shouldn't go in October."

Shaun pointed excitedly to the top of the mountains. "Look, Jade, snow! Bet you'd like to get your satchel out and sketch that! And look at all the campfires," he breathed in awe.

She glanced at the large company of silver seekers on their way to Virginia City. Horses and mules were tied to brush and trees, and men sat hunched before their small fires eating from tin plates. She knew some had stopped here only for the night, others to wait for the arrival of mule trains to take them over the Sierras into the Nevada territory.

"This is a horrible place," Holly whispered, glancing around. "I don't see any women, and I certainly don't see Pa."

"It's been six years. We'd hardly recognize him. He may have a beard."

"Oh, Jade, lets go back to Placerville and wait for Pa there. What's your vote, Shaun?"

Shaun glanced silently from Holly to Jade, then pulled his hat lower over his eyes and looked down at his black boots.

"We can't go back," Jade stated. "We have a few cents to buy some supper tonight and that's all. And look! There're some women over there."

"They're wearing men's trousers. And look at their faces—painted like a firehouse. We should have written Aunt Norma in New York. Mama always said her sister had a grand house and—"

"We've been through this a dozen times, Holly. Mama's sister wouldn't have anything to do with her after she married a Southerner. And with talk of civil war, do you think she'd have anything to do with us now?"

"It wasn't because Mama married Pa. It's because she

8

became a Christian. Even Pa got mad and called her a fanatic—"

"It was both reasons," Jade cut in quickly. "Anyway, Aunt Norma's never laid eyes on us," said Jade, straightening Shaun's blue jacket, and giving him a reassuring smile. "Goodness, Holly! We can't just show up on her front porch with no money and all our baggage now, can we?"

"And don't forget Keeper," Shaun hastened to add, tightening his hold on the kitten. "He'll need to be fed at least his supper. Maybe our Yankee aunt wouldn't give him any. Keeper's a Reb. Besides, I want to see some Indians."

At least Norma has a house." Holly sighed wistfully. "Mama said when she was a girl she had her own bedroom. Think what it would be like, Jade, a whole closet to yourself just stuffed with beautiful ball dresses! Here, it's going to be awful. The man in Placerville said the alkali dust gets in your mouth and ears and seeps through your skin. Ugh! With you getting sick all the time, and never knowing when you'll need a doctor—"

Jade turned on her with blazing green eyes, her jaw set stubbornly. "Don't start that again. I don't want to hear it. I'm not ill! Not anymore!"

Holly was in no mood to back down. She was tired and cranky. "You are, too! And why is it I can say anything and you don't get mad until I mention your illness?"

"Because I'm not ill!"

"You don't fool me, Jade. You're putting on an act. Even now you're pale. Isn't she, Shaun?"

Shaun frowned, keeping his dark head bent, and ran his fingers through Keeper's soft fur. "Keeper's heart is pounding." With his other hand Shaun tied the rope more securely to his belt. "If Keeper darts off into the pine trees I won't be able to find him. Some bear will get him."

"Jade's ill, isn't she?" Holly pressed the boy.

Jade knew that Shaun was loyal to her. Of his two sisters she was his favorite because she understood his fears. She was also sympathetic about the cat, and Holly hadn't wanted to let him bring it.

"It must be awful to spend months in bed the way Jade has," Shaun said quietly. "What would I do all that time? Why, even Keeper would get bored and go out the window."

Holly folded her arms, and her blue eyes scanned her sister worriedly. "Dr. Kelsey said the disease is dormant, but it can come back any time. You ought to admit it, Jade."

"Hush, that man with the beard is looking at us."

"They all have beards. Crawling with fleas, no doubt, and I've never seen a meaner looking lot."

Jade agreed, but wouldn't admit it. The men looked alike. They all wore beards, their hair was long, their rugged faces were bronzed from the summer sun, and each man carried his weapons: a rifle, or a gun at his hip, and somewhere, a knife.

"This is where we should be, with our father," said Jade.

"Indeed? What makes you think he wants us?" the voice was a little bitter.

Jade quickly glanced from Holly to Shaun and saw him wince. She nudged Holly's foot with the toe of her shoe. The warning stare told her to be silent. But it was true. Jade knew that Thomas O'Neil was a gambler,

10

and some said even a gunslinger, but Jade refused to believe the latter. She changed the subject to their Uncle Samuel.

"Samuel will be in Virginia City, too. If the Lord sent him to teach the Scriptures, why wouldn't it be right for us to come and help him?"

"Pa will strike it rich in silver," added Shaun. "Then you'll be glad we came."

"Oh, sure. And until he does we'll be cramped together in a one room cabin in a mining camp. How are we going to wash—and cook? Where does the food come from? And what of our nice clothes? And what if you end up in bed again, Jade? With the Sierras snowed in and Virginia City isolated until spring, there won't be a doctor!"

"I don't want to talk about it," Jade said stiffly.

"And I know why. Since Beau wouldn't marry a girl who's sick, you're trying to prove something to yourself at our expense."

The flicker of pain in Jade's eyes said that Holly had touched a raw wound.

"Coming here won't change the reason he wouldn't marry you. If anything, you'll grow worse. Dr. Kelsey said so."

Jade flushed, remembering the letter from Beau Wilson's father, which had arrived at the height of her illness. Mr. Wilson had explained to her mother why Beau, who had been accepted to serve as a missionary to the Indians in Texas, must break the engagement.

"Beau is in no position to take on an ailing young bride. What if her illness forces him to neglect the ministry in order to care for her, or even resign and return to St. Louis? And what if children are born to be left motherless at the age of two or three?

11

"We sadly join with the mission board to confess that we do not believe this marriage is advisable. And so. . . ."

The reasons were logical, but the rejection was none the less painful. A tornado had ripped through her life's plans leaving them in rubble.

"God will grant the grace to carry on until you're well again," her mother had tried to comfort her.

Until she was well. . . .

The words echoed in Jade's mind like mocking laughter. Until. . . .

Summer had turned to fall, and the leaves had become gold and brown, followed by the new green of spring, then the gray of winter.

Until. . . .

Jade wouldn't admit it openly, but she believed that whatever purpose God had for her life would be too small to satisfy her restless yearnings. She wanted to prove her circumstances wrong. "I'm well enough to serve the Lord as a missionary among the Indians—if not with Beau in Texas, then with Uncle Samuel in Nevada," she had told herself.

But now as she stood facing Holly, Jade feared to admit how fatigued she felt, or that there were the familiar twinges of discomfort in her lungs.

The cold wind bit into her flesh and sent the curls fluttering under her green bonnet. She became aware of Shaun's hand clutching her arm, his eyes wide as he looked up at her. She was now all the mother he had, and she must be strong. She could no longer be the little girl who sought comfort, but the source of strength and courage for her brother and sister.

She brought Shaun against her with a little hug. "It's all right," she whispered. "Don't pay any attention to

Holly. She's tired. I'm not going to get sick again."

And to herself Jade thought, *I won't be a burden here in Virginia City. . . .Somehow, with God's help, I'll make it. I must.*

Again she glanced about. She first must find their father among the crowd of miners. Whatever would she do stranded in Strawberry with Holly, Shaun, and a cat? Jade faced her first obstacle and was determined to get over it.

She reached into her carrying bag. "Here, divide this between you."

She handed them the last gingerbread cake and a small jug of milk that had grown a little sour since leaving Placerville. The peace offering was enough to humor Shaun but not Holly.

"Now what?" Holly demanded.

"Wait here," said Jade. "I'm going into the tavern. Maybe Pa left a message with the proprietor."

"It's a saloon! And they're all men!"

Jade raised her chin. "So? They can't all be thieves and fools."

"Mama would have a fit seeing you traipsing about without a chaperon."

"The situation demands it. Please, Holly, just do as I ask? Wait here."

"Oh, all right, but don't say I didn't tell you so when some old goat makes a remark."

Jade gathered her muslin skirt and eased her way in the direction of the wooden structure, cautiously avoiding the thickest part of the crowd. The lovely figure in the yards of green muslin with the matching feather in her bonnet turned the eyes of many. Some gaped at her, startled, as if confronting a blossom in the broiling desert sun, but a few stepped out of her way in

13

deference, and went so far as to tip their hats.

"Evenin', Miss."

"You watch them chug holes, Ma'am."

Jade nodded silently and walked on. The rumpus grew louder as she neared the structure. Within, she heard the plucking of a banjo and many voices rising and falling. The place was packed to the door.

Near the freight platform she saw heavily loaded mule trains. She guessed that the precious commodities of flour, coffee, side bacon, beans, and blankets were being brought into Virginia City before the winter snows isolated the mining town until spring.

The boisterous men were hollering back and forth, as she neared, but all Jade heard were the words 'silver,' 'blue-stuff,' 'veins,' 'rich-ore.' Her eyes drifted to a wagon stopped not far away. A young woman sat in back. There was a hard expression on her lean, brown face, and her thin lips were drawn tight. Straight black hair fell about her shoulders, and her dark eyes were unsmiling.

Is she Indian? wondered Jade. A rifle lay across her knees. Jade felt the sullen stare fix like hungry flies on her green muslin dress with its trim of eggshell lace. Sensing her resentment, Jade turned her head to read the sign that hung out over the yard on timber aged by the seasons.

Berry's Tavern.

Should she go inside? If she was to find her father, she must.

Chapter 2

The stained canvas siding of Berry's Tavern shook in the October wind. The makeshift counter that stretched across some rough barrels was crowded with men two and three deep. Roark Montgomery stood just inside the door for a moment, watching. He removed his black hat and ran his fingers through his dark hair. His eyes calmly scanned the faces of the crowd, missing nothing. The man he sought would be difficult to identify. When he had last trailed him through Texas and into Missouri, he hadn't worn a beard. The question was, would O'Neil ride into Strawberry Flat to meet the gunmen he had hired out of Utah?

Roark recognized the three gunslingers across the heads of other men at the counter. Their eyes locked with his before they turned away as if they didn't see him.

Men stepped aside, making room as Roark walked

up and rested his elbow on the counter. "Well, well, if it isn't the Mandel brothers."

A wiry young man with cat-like movements nudged the man next to him and stuttered, "H-hey, Jesse, it's M-Montgomery!"

Jesse Mandel turned his head, and his hard black eyes narrowed as he met Roark's even stare. Roark lounged easily against the counter, unintimidated. "Going to Virginia City to prospect, or to offer your gun for hire?"

"Don't see it's any of your business, Montgomery. Your badge don't give you no authority in Washoe. Nevada ain't even a state."

"J-just the w-way we like it, M-Montgomery," stuttered the other with a grin.

Roark lifted a brow. "Ernie, when are you going to take my advice? Stop following your brother Jesse into trouble. One of these days Jesse's going to get you killed."

Ernie frowned. "J-Jesse's always b-been smarter than me. Wouldn't know h-how to make it with-without him." He turned to a third man standing with them. "A-ain't that right, Letterman? W-we need Jesse, don't w-we?"

"Shut up, Ernie, your stuttering gets on my nerves," said Letterman cruelly. "I don't need nobody." He turned slowly, moving his jacket away from his hip. He measured Roark with an icy stare. The tense moment of silence was broken when he said, "So you're the lawman from 'Frisco I've been hearin' about. Seems to me I've been hearin' too much recently, Montgomery. It's startin' to get on my nerves somethin' awful."

Roark appeared undisturbed, even amused. "Looks to me like you've got yourself a chronic case of nerves,

Letterman. I can't do much about Ernie, but I can advise you to ride back to Salt Lake. My reputation doesn't reach that far—yet."

Letterman's jaw tightened; then, he gave a soft laugh and smiled thinly. "Heard say you don't rile easy, but then, neither do I. Heard say you carry a little black book with you beneath those San Francisco duds."

Letterman's eyes were fixed on Roark. "Heard say you're good with that Colt of yours."

A slight smile played on Roark's mouth. "You heard right."

"Heard say you took Skinner at Placerville before he even aimed."

Roark's gaze was unreadable under dark lashes, but his eyes read every movement of the gunslinger's hand. "That's right."

The man's face hardened. "Better be careful, Montgomery. I could beat Skinner left-handed. I might just help my reputation by getting rid of a San Francisco lawman. I could take you now, nice and easy like, and there ain't no one here good enough to stop me."

Roark sighed. "Pride is a cruel master with a greedy appetite. Some say it can't be satisfied. Don't let it provoke you into an act of folly, Letterman. I've no desire to add your name to my reputation. But I will, if you've a yearning to be buried here on Strawberry Flat."

"Back off, Letterman," snapped Jesse. "He's right. I got no hankerin' for trouble, not now, hear?"

Fury filled Letterman's face, but he seemed unsure enough to be cautious.

Jesse glared at Roark. "Look here, Montgomery, what d'ya want with me and Ernie?"

17

"Got one question to ask you. Where's Thomas O'Neil?"

Jesse looked at his brother Ernie. "You ever heard of Thomas O'Neil?"

"Not me, Jesse. You h-heard of him?"

Jesse turned back to Montgomery with a slight sneer. "Ain't it a shame? We ain't never heard of the man."

"It was a bad night on that boat in San Francisco. Remember, Jesse?"

Jesse and his brother stiffened.

"An innocent bystander was shot during that card game. You sure you haven't seen Thomas O'Neil?"

Jesse's eyes flickered with uncertainty. His jaw twitched nervously.

"I had nothing to do with that night on the boat. And we don't know any Thomas O'Neil. We don't hang around gamblers." He smirked. "What do you take us for, Montgomery? Common thieves?" He puffed a stubby cigar.

Ernie laughed. "H-hey that's a g-good one, Jesse!"

Roark casually pushed the cigar away. "If I were you, Jesse, I'd find a healthier habit. I'd also go back to Salt Lake. Virginia City's going to get a little crowded. A little unhealthy for fast guns. Your gun, Jesse.

"I hear Thomas is there. I'm under authority from Governor Downey to bring him back for trial. You see, one of the innocent men who was shot that night was a friend of the Governor's, a good friend." Roark paused, then added smoothly, "He was my friend, too, Jesse. He was my father."

The moment tensed. Jesse's Adam's apple bobbed up and down as he swallowed. A glance passed between the three men.

"You got nothing on us, Montgomery. We had nothing to do with that night in 'Frisco."

"Then stay out of my way in Virginia City."

"What makes you think we intend to get in your way?"

"Because Thomas is there. He might be interested in jumping someone's claim—like he tried to do at Sutter's in California. You remember that, too, don't you, Jesse? You were there when the miner was shot in the back. I was so sure you were there. I just couldn't find the witness. Strange. He's still missing. I wonder where he could be?"

"Don't know what you're rantin' about. I ain't killed no witness. And I don't know nothin' about jumpin' a claim in Virginia City."

"Don't mix with Thomas again, Jesse. California was a bad mistake. Take Ernie and go home to Utah."

Jesse said nothing, neither did his brother Ernie.

Letterman stood, his face hard, his clear eyes like ice. "I don't know anything about 'Frisco, or Sutter's Mill. I do know this sounds like a threat. Doesn't it sound to you like a threat, Jesse?"

"Jesse doesn't think so," said Roark smoothly. "Do you, Jesse?"

Jesse swallowed. "Who me? Naw, no threat, Letterman." He nudged his brother Ernie with his elbow. "Let's go."

Letterman stared at Roark Montgomery. "I don't like threats, San Francisco lawman."

"Your two friends were wise enough to pass on it. I'd be unhappy if I thought you weren't as smart as Ernie."

Letterman's hand shook with a barely suppressed

fury. For a moment he seemed about to draw, but Roark Montgomery's even stare unnerved him. Letterman was dangerous, but he was also cautious. He turned and walked out with the other two.

The main room was packed, and the incident passed unnoticed. Catching Berry's attention, Roark waved a greeting. Going behind the counter, Berry tossed him a tin mug.

"Well, Montgomery, what brings you here? Got a mind for stumblin' over a pot o' silver at Washoe?"

Roark held out the tin cup. "I'll settle for some of that coffee."

Berry filled the cup. "A San Franciscan gentleman who enjoys my coffee is a right nice compliment. Say. . ." he leaned toward him and said in a low voice, "I hear you're lookin' for a man."

"Ever heard of Thomas O'Neil?"

"There's a cantankerous person workin' among the placer miners in Virginny town. Name's Samuel O'Neil, but ain't never heard of any Thomas. Expectin' trouble?"

"The usual amount. Anyone passing through mention O'Neil?"

"Got more wanted guns passin' through than I've seen in all the years I've been on the Sierras. No doubt this Thomas O'Neil's done passed through. I must've fed ten thousand since news of silver last year—" He stopped suddenly as an argument broke out. Berry set his pot down and shouldered his way through the crowd, intending to boot them both out before they got into a fight.

The heat and odor in the room was unbearable, so Roark took his tin cup and stepped out into the cold wind.

There was the feel of snow in the blowing gusts sweeping down from the Sierras. He lifted the cup to drink, but paused when he caught sight of a girl in a green, flowing dress. He watched her. Where had he seen her before? Every blink of dark lash spoke her shock as she drew closer to the saloon, but it seemed quickly overcome by sheer determination.

Nice. In fact. . .very nice. But much too young. He drank his coffee. She was obviously unprepared for Strawberry Flat. She looked to have just escaped her grandmother's parlor for the first time.

All at once there were shouts from within and the crash of splintering wood. Roark calmly stepped away from the door, holding his coffee cup so it wouldn't spill.

The girl's wide green eyes stared in disbelief as a man sailed through the door and landed in the mud in front of her, followed by his black hat.

A girl with a rifle jumped down from the wagon and walked to where the middle-aged man lay sprawled. Unlike the girl in flowing green, this girl did not appear shocked. In fact, she looked as if she had expected it, as if it might have happened on numerous occasions. She snatched up the hat and knocked flecks of dirt off, then placed it solidly on the man's head. In another minute she was helping him to his feet.

"You all in one piece, Pa?"

"No good Yankee!" the man grumbled in his beard.

"Pa! Throw that tarantula juice away! Someday it'll kill you." As she struggled to get the bottle of whiskey from his clutch, a wrestling match ensued.

Just then, Jade glanced up toward the tavern door,

21

and her eyes collided with Roark Montgomery, leaning his shoulder against the building. She realized that he had been watching her reaction to the scene, and there was a look of amusement on his face. He smiled.

He stood aloof from the others, a loner, and a stranger to their greed. He was unlike the miners; there was a different spirit about him. First, he wore no beard, a sure sign that he did not belong. His clothes, too, spoke sophistication and were well tailored. He was young—and quite handsome.

She noticed his height and strength at once, perhaps because her own faltering health heightened her awareness of strength in others. She blushed at her thoughts.

And yet—she couldn't tear her eyes away. The man looked overwhelming, and her eyes narrowed with an abrupt decision to dislike what she saw. Too masculine. Too reckless. No man who looked like that could be of any spiritual consequence, she decided. No doubt he was a gunslinger or a gambler from San Francisco. Yes, that must be it, a gambler! Why, look at his clothes and—

Realizing that she was staring, Jade turned her head away and caught her breath. Too late, he had started toward her.

This is the last thing I need. Jade told herself, her heart pounding. She picked up her skirts to rush across the yard between the wagons, but a driver's shout halted her.

"Ho! Miss! Easy there! You'll get yerself killed!"

She was blocked by a mule who took that moment to decide that he didn't like his new route and brayed. Jade stiffened as she heard the stranger come up behind her.

22

"Never again will I lose my temper with a mule. This one has made our meeting possible," came the amused voice.

She tried to place his accent. It was not Southern, but neither did it have the Eastern twang.

"You look lost," he continued smoothly. "Perhaps I can be of help."

Her face flushed over her predicament. "You are wrong, sir. I am far from being lost."

She turned, prepared to face a dragon spewing godless fire and smoke. Instead, she saw hair as dark as her own, eyes a stormy blue-gray gazing down from under black lashes, and a narrow mustache that lined his upper lip. Jade immediately sensed that his appearance was not the most striking thing about him. What she had noticed from afar came to her with striking clarity as she stared up at him. His eyes glinted with an uncompromising inner strength that arrested her attention and left her disarmed. The face of Beau Wilson instantly dimmed into a feeble shadow.

He towered over her by at least a foot, dressed in a fine dark jacket over a leather vest, well-fitted trousers of good quality, and heavy boots. Her eyes faltered downward to the gun peeping out from under the jacket near his hip.

"The name is Roark Montgomery."

Jade struggled to resist the unexpected barrage against her emotions. She reacted in self-defense by responding too coolly.

"Indeed?"

Did she sound as disinterested as she intended?"

She turned her head and looked about as if expecting to see someone. She hoped Roark Montgomery would walk on, but he watched her.

"Looking for your father?"

"Why—yes, but how did you know?"

"Now who else would a little girl be looking for?"

Little girl! Jade was stung. Her eyes opened wide in indignation, then she wondered why his evaluation should irritate her so. Perhaps I'm looking for my husband, she almost quipped, but did not.

"My first impression of you, Miss—?" and Roark Montgomery paused.

If he's waiting for me to introduce myself, he'll be disappointed, she thought. Her green eyes turned cool when she read the contained amusement in the expression of his mouth.

He smiled slightly, then went on with little break in his voice, "—Is that you're too young to be hanging around a place like this alone."

Jade felt herself being challenged by the blue-gray eyes staring down at her. A feeling of resistance began to churn. He was older than she was and appeared to be experienced with life's worst situations, but she was far from being a child.

"Where's your guardian?" he asked.

That did it!

"I need no guardian, sir. I can take care of myself, thank you."

A slight smile told her he was not disturbed by her retort, only amused. "As you wish." He tipped his hat, and Jade swept past.

She walked to the tavern door and was about to pass through when she felt a hand grab her arm.

"You, Missy, gotta minute?" came a raspy voice.

Jade stiffened and jerked her arm away. Her eyes fell on a burly man who had been watching her.

24

"No." She started to side step. He stepped in front of her with a leer that showed teeth stained by tobacco and leaned closer. His breath smelled of liquor.

"Missy, you alone?"

"Get out of my way."

"You can get rich on the Washoe if you listen to my offer."

"I'm not interested. You're in my way, sir!"

"I got just the job for you, Missy. You and I can go into business together. Between us, we'll make more money than those who own feet on the richest claim on the Comstock."

Her skin crawled at the evil gleam in his eye. "I told you I wasn't interested," and she tried to brush past him.

"Now wait here Miss High 'n Mighty—"

"You heard her," came a toneless voice.

Jade glanced aside, and saw Roark Montgomery. Her breath escaped with a sigh of relief. Irritated by the interruption, the man sputtered angrily. "You telling me what to do—"

"I am. Keep moving."

The man turned back to Jade. He reached out and grabbed her arm again. "Now, Missy—"

Roark took the front of the man's vest and effortlessly pulled him forward. "She's not interested. Keep your hands off." He gave him a shove. The man stumbled backward and landed seat down in the mud. Roark took her elbow and propelled her through the onlookers who parted for them.

Jade kept her eyes straight ahead, hoping her blush wasn't showing. "It appears I'm in your debt."

"I don't collect debts from young girls. I'll escort you

back to your guardian before you get into worse trouble."

"I appreciate your gallantry just now, Mr. Montgomery, but I am not a child who has escaped her Nanny."

Roark laughed, and Jade hastened to add, "I am my own guardian, sir."

"Indeed?" he appeared amused.

"My father's a miner in Virginia City. I wrote him from Placerville that we'd arrive today. We expect him to meet us."

"We? Then someone is with you?"

"My sister and little brother."

His dark brow slanted upward. "I suppose you're their guardian as well? May I ask when you sent the letter?"

"Three weeks ago."

"Then your father should have received it. But I'd like to give you a word of advice," and his gaze came to rest on the green feather in her bonnet. "There's nothing in Virginia City for a girl like you. Ideals are bartered away cheaply here. I've seen men throw away a fortune in one night. I've seen others shoot a man, then order supper. The lure of easy riches, and the ability to enforce a man's own pioneer justice has whetted the appetite of too many. If I were you, I'd catch the first stage back to Placerville. If you like, I can send word to your father."

There came that big brother tone in his voice again, she thought. It was time to tell him flat out what her intentions were.

"I knew what Virginia City offered before I left St. Louis. My uncle is a circuit riding preacher working with the miners and the Indians, and I intend to help him."

There wasn't the slightest snag in his poise. He looked her over from head to toe without appearing to do so.

"I'm pleased the Lord means so much to you. There aren't too many of us around who know how worthy He is of our faith and service."

Jade almost choked.

"But I still think you should take the stage back down the mountain," he said silkily and smiled.

The expression on his handsome face did little to ease her shock, or make her feel more comfortable. She was grateful that he knew the Lord, but he remained a masculine risk where her feelings were concerned. There was something about him that strongly attracted her, yet he gave the impression of being unreachable. She had the feeling that Roark Montgomery could prove more painful to her heart than even Beau Wilson. Too risky, much too risky. She glanced about for her father with a confidence she did not feel, but wanted him to think she did.

His eyes didn't waver. "The Indians can be vicious when they get riled. My grandmother was scalped by the Piutes."

Scalped! Her eyes darted back to his. Jade swallowed, and her hand automatically touched her hair.

He said smoothly, "A Piute would set a high price on curls like that."

"Mr. Montgomery, you're trying to frighten me."

"Now why would I do that?" His voice breathed with innocence.

Her lashes narrowed. "I've the notion you don't want me to go to Virginia City, and I don't know why. We're complete strangers."

"Christians are never complete strangers to each other. But you're right, I don't think you should go to Virginia City. My dear, I've a feeling you don't know what you're getting yourself into."

Jade drew in a breath. "Am I so dimwitted, sir? Or do you believe every woman is incapable of knowing what she's 'getting herself into'?"

"If a woman's going to serve the Lord among the Piutes, she should have a husband to back her up with a shotgun."

"The Lord's quite able to protect me without a shotgun."

"He is. He also expects us to use some good common sense. My grandmother decided to journey out to the Forty-Mile Desert near the Humboldt River. My grandfather was there doing some mission work. There were signal fires all over the ridge. The Piutes were angered over a killing done by a passing wagon train. Need I tell you what happened during the assembly?"

"No," she said flatly. "I get the idea."

"No angels came to intervene. I was a boy then. I watched the whole thing and was helpless to stop it. So you see, I have this problem with green eyes and ebony curls riding a lone mule out to the Forty-Mile."

Quickly she discovered that Roark Montgomery was a determined man when it came to what he believed. He was also too domineering, she decided, and perhaps a bit conceited.

"I'm sorry about your grandmother, but I've no intention of riding out alone when the signal fires are sending war messages on the hills."

"I don't think your uncle will be any more at ease with your plans than I am. You said your father is a

28

miner. Does he also help your uncle?"

Jade felt her heart sink. As far back as she could remember, Thomas O'Neil had mocked Christianity and had brought much distress to her mother. There was also gossip of something even worse than his gambling—something that had taken place while her father was on one of the riverboats steaming across San Francisco Bay. Just what it was, Jade had not been able to discover. She wasn't sure she wanted to know. Having nothing good to say of her father, Jade changed the subject.

"So far, Mr. Montgomery, it's you who has asked all the questions. Besides your name and knowing you're a Christian, just why should I listen to you?"

"Perhaps this will make you feel easier about my questions—and my advice." He reached into his pocket and pulled out a small metal badge. "I've a natural tendency to get involved. Especially when I see a young girl about to take the wrong road."

Jade felt a little foolish, and also relieved.

"I suppose you took me for a fast-gun?"

"Actually. . .a gambler."

He arched his brows.

"My apology, Mr. Montgomery."

"Roark, not Mister."

"Then you're a lawman in Virginia City?"

"San Francisco."

That accounted for his manners and nice dress, she decided, trying not to scan him again. "My name is Jade."

"Your eyes, no doubt?"

The blush came too easily under his stare. "What?"

"A man would need to be blind to miss those green

eyes. They explain the name of Jade."

"Oh."

Jade was angry with herself for the lack of poise. No wonder he took her for a child when all she could do was blush and stammer. She fumbled with her bonnet and dragged her eyes from his. "Yes, my mother decided on the name."

Just then Shaun and Holly shouted, and they both turned.

"Jade!"

Shaun ran up, his large, expressive eyes were wide as they stared up at Roark Montgomery with quick devotion. "Hi, I'm Shaun. That man over there said you were a lawman! Can I see your badge?"

"Shaun," said Jade, embarrassed, but Roark readily obliged him by sitting down on his haunches and handing him the badge. Jade glanced at Holly. She was staring at Roark with her lips parted a little. Jade gave her a nudge. Holly's mouth closed, and she straightened her shoulders.

Shaun was showing Roark his cat. "He sure could use a little milk," he said, and glanced hopefully at Jade. "That ginger cake didn't help me much either." His eyes wandered toward the tavern where the smell of food drifted out on the cold wind.

Jade thought of the few cents remaining in her purse. It appeared as if her father had forgotten to show up. If she spent their money on supper and a night's lodging, how would she get them to Virginia City?

She frowned, and, looking up, saw Roark watching her. Did he guess she had little money? He directed his question, however, to Shaun, and Jade believed he did so deliberately to keep her from being able to refuse.

"Are you as hungry as I am?"

Shaun's eyes brightened. "Yes sir!"

"I think it's time we all had something to eat. Come on."

Jade wanted to protest but saw that she had lost Shaun's attention. The boy was already in a state of hero worship of the lawman from San Francisco.

Chapter 3

Inside Berry's Tavern it was hot and stuffy. Jade wanted to hold a handkerchief over her nose. Holly nudged her and whispered, "Now what are we going to do? Pa's not here, and it's almost dark."

Berry glanced up and saw Roark Montgomery again. "Looks like you got your hands full, Montgomery. What'll ya have?"

"Whatever you've got."

"Beef 'n beans."

"We'll take it."

Shaun spoke up intently. "Sir? Make that five plates? And the fifth one fill with cream?"

Berry looked down at him. "Cream?"

Roark smiled and reached over to open the boy's coat. Keeper's two big gold eyes stared back.

"Meow?"

"Sorry, lad, I ain't got no milk, how about a saucer of gravy?"

"Oh that will do fine, sir. Keeper likes gravy, especially chicken gravy."

"He'll have to settle for beef," said Berry wryly.

Roark gestured inquiringly toward the kitchen.

"Sure, Montgomery. Take 'em on back."

As Roark turned away, Berry leaned toward him and said quietly, "The man you asked about earlier? Just came to me sudden like. Heard he passed on into Placerville a few days ago."

Jade hadn't meant to overhear, but now she wondered. So Roark was looking for a man. A gunslinger, perhaps? She glanced at him sideways. One thing was sure, he would have no difficulty taking care of himself.

There was a roughly hewn wooden table in the cooking area with a little privacy. Jade loosened the ties of her bonnet and set it aside.

Now that she sat down and there was a lull, she became aware of how exhausted she was. Her heart pounded with odd little jerks and her head ached. She hated to admit it, but the grueling trip up the mountain from Placerville had taken its toll. The room became too hot, too tight, and for a moment appeared to move unsteadily. She felt unmasked, as if everyone could tell she was ill. The thought made her feel ashamed and brought a tight feeling of fear. No one must know, especially Roark Montgomery.

"Coffee?" she heard him ask.

"Please."

He stood up to get them a cup. When he was out of hearing, Holly glared. "So, how do we reach Virginia City, Miss Know-it-all?"

"You mean Pa isn't coming?" whispered Shaun.

"Don't worry, I'll take care of it. We'll reach him somehow."

Roark returned with the hot coffee, and she smiled her thanks. The proprietor brought their plates. One whiff and Jade nearly gagged. She couldn't possibly eat this!

"Is there another stage tonight for Virginia City?"

"There ain't no stage." He set the plate before her. "From here you go by mule."

Jade felt the pressure of Holly's foot beneath the bench as she registered her complaint. Ignoring her, Jade inquired calmly, "And where do we get mules?"

"Didn't you buy tickets in Placerville before getting on the stage?"

"What tickets?" spoke up Holly with a scowl. "You mean we have to buy more tickets?"

Jade was embarrassed. "When do the mules leave?"

"Don't rightly know. Early." He turned to Roark who had remained silent. "Wylet will be coming in from Carson City. They can get a ride from him."

"Wylet?" asked Jade.

"A friend of mine," said Roark. "He owns and runs several mule trains in and out of Nevada."

The plate of beans and chunks of beef stared up at Jade. Each tiny swallow seemed to lump in her throat. They were spicy and hot and made her eyes water. Quickly she took a swallow of the coffee and fanned herself with her bonnet.

Roark stood and picked up his hat. "You'll need to camp here tonight. I'll ask Berry to keep an eye on you until Wylet arrives with the mules."

Did that mean he wasn't going to Virginia City? Jade wondered. She couldn't bring herself to inquire and was grateful when Shaun blurted out, "But, Montgomery! I mean, Mister. Aren't you coming, too?"

Afraid not, son; I need to return to Placerville tonight."

"When will you come back?"

"I don't know that I will."

Shaun's eyes dropped to Montgomery's holster.

"Are you looking for a badman?"

"Don't ask so many questions, Shaun; it isn't polite," said Jade, but she, too, was curious.

"Sure you won't change your mind, and go back? I'll see you into Placerville," he said.

She looked up, and for a moment it seemed that the blue-gray irises could fill her entire world. He was so masculine, so easy to look at, that she lowered her head and picked up the fork. Anything to hide the disturbing thoughts racing through her mind. Again she felt Holly nudge her beneath the table with her foot, this time a little harder. Again Jade refused to cooperate.

"I'm quite sure, Mr. Montgomery. Thank you for supper, though, and for your concern."

He seemed to hesitate, then—"There's something I'd like to do before I leave, if you don't mind. I'd like to pray with the three of you. It isn't often I meet Christians, and you are in a rather tight situation until your father arrives. Would you mind?"

"Of course not, I'd like that," she said, and her voice broke a little. No one had prayed with them since the death of their mother the previous year, least of all a man. Shaun's eyes shone as his impression of the

35

lawman grew a foot taller, and with gravity he bowed his head. Only Holly blushed.

When he had finished, he left, and Jade looked at her supper plate, now cold. The table was silent, and she sensed a strange emptiness already setting in. A glimpse at Shaun told her that he was disappointed.

"I hope he comes back. Do you think he will, Jade?"

Jade pushed his plate closer to him. "I don't know. I doubt it. Finish up. We won't eat again soon." She offered a smile of sympathy. "Maybe tomorrow we'll see Pa and Uncle Samuel."

Unexpectedly, Holly grabbed her tin cup and started out. "I want some more of that coffee. I'll be right back."

As Roark walked out of the tavern, he spied Berry ladling a plate full of food. He leaned across the counter and pressed money into Berry's hand. "This is for your trouble. Keep an eye on them. They'll be here until Wylet arrives. Tell him to make sure they reach Carson."

"Will do, Montgomery."

The gusts of wind were turning icy as he walked to the stable. Would he find Thomas O'Neil in Placerville?

The sky was ebony; the white stars gleamed like pieces of crystal, but in the east he saw clouds that promised a storm. Rough weather ahead. He saddled his horse in the stable and led it across the yard toward the trail. He was ready to mount when he heard someone running and a girl's voice.

"Oh, Mr. Montgomery?"

Holly ran up, breathless. "I was wondering if I—if I

could impose on you a little further?"

Roark smiled to himself as he saw her fluster. "Of course, Holly. What can I do for you?"

"Well—" she cleared her throat. "We have an aunt in New York, but Jade will have a fit if she learns I've written to her asking for help. But if someone else notified her of our situation, maybe Jade would change her mind about going there."

"Do you mind telling me what's wrong with your sister? She's ill."

"Oh dear, she'll be mad at me if I say anything."

Roark pressed her smoothly. "Has she been ill for long?"

Holly glanced over her shoulder to Berry's Flat. "The truth is, Dr. Kelsey said it was consumption."

There was silence. He muttered something then said, "I should have guessed. How long has she had it?"

"Jade's spent half her life in and out of bed, Mr. Montgomery. That's where she learned to sketch and paint. Dr. Kelsey doesn't think she'll ever get well. It comes and goes, and—"

"I understand tuberculosis. My father is a physician. And so she's come *here*?" His voice was quiet but revealed a strain of anger. "Does she know what the winters are like here? And the alkali dust is enough to clog a man's nostrils and parch his lungs!"

Roark was attentive as Holly explained about their mother, the broken engagement, and the house in St. Louis. "We only had two choices," she concluded, "Our aunt in New York or Virginia City. Jade insisted we come here to find our Pa. She intends to do some art sketches and sell them to an Eastern newspaper or magazine. And, she has a few things to prove to herself."

Roark took a dislike to the image of Beau Wilson. "I see. By the way, how long was she engaged to this Beau?"

"Two years."

"That's quite a long time for a girl of sixteen," he said smoothly, knowing that she was older.

"Sixteen? Jade? She's twenty-two."

He smiled slightly. "She's still in love with him?"

Holly shrugged. "With Jade it's hard to tell. I always thought she was more in love with the idea of being a missionary to the Texas Indians than she was with Beau."

"Why do you think so?"

"Oh. . .because there was never any—well, you know, romance between them, if you know what I mean. Oh dear, Jade's going to kill me. . . ."

Roark smiled. "Yes, I do know what you mean about romance, Holly. And I'll be happy to send a wire to your aunt. Do you have her New York address?"

"I've got it right here." She handed him a folded piece of paper. "Oh, how can I thank you?"

"No need to thank me. I'll have your aunt write your father. What's his name?"

"Thomas O'Neil."

Roark Montgomery stopped short. He stared down at Holly, stunned.

"Is—is something wrong?" she stammered.

He said nothing. He could not have spoken if he'd wanted to. His lips sealed tightly and his jaw clenched. It couldn't be!

"Well—I—I better get back," Holly said uneasily. "Thank you for your help, Mr. Montgomery. Good-bye."

"Wait!"

38

Holly stopped and turned. Roark gripped his horse's reins.

"Your father is Thomas O'Neil from St. Louis?"

"Yes. You've heard of him?"

"Seen him lately?"

"No, not for the last six years."

Six years, he thought. Then Thomas thought nothing of neglecting his family.

"He didn't even show for mama's funeral," Holly said.

Roark noticed that her voice had grown bitter.

He said nothing more. What could he say? How could he tell them he was going to arrest their father for killing two men? He stood there silently and watched Holly run back toward the tavern.

Jade was waiting with a knowing scowl when Holly came into Berry's kitchen and sat down at the table.

"Did you go running after Roark Montgomery?"

"What if I did? He's the only friend we have."

"Did you tell him about me?"

"What if I did? Why's it such a big secret? You act as if being sick is being criminal!"

"It's a personal matter, that's all. Can't you understand that? It's not something I want shouted about to just anybody."

"Roark Montgomery isn't just anybody. He's a Christian, a lawman, and he bought our supper."

"You told him what Dr. Kelsey said, didn't you? And about Beau breaking the engagement!" Jade jumped to her feet, feeling humiliated. "Holly, how could you!"

Holly squirmed. "Honestly, Jade, so what? He won't be back."

"You don't know that. He might decide to come back. Didn't he say that the mule train driver is his friend? What did he say when you told him about my illness?"

"The same thing I've been telling you since we left St. Louis. Did you know his father's a doctor?"

Surprised, Jade scanned her face. "Did he tell you that?"

"He sure did behave strangely about Pa, though."

"Oh? Why is that?"

"I don't know, but when I said his name, he looked as if, well, almost as if I'd slapped him."

Their eyes met. Suddenly a horrid thought came to Jade. She forgot her own embarrassment. Suppose. . . suppose being a lawman, Roark Montgomery was looking for Thomas O'Neil? No. It couldn't be, Jade's mind denied the thought.

Jade shuddered and tore her eyes from Holly's for fear her sister would read her dark thoughts. There was nothing to warrant her suspicions, and it had been a trying day. There was no need to add to Holly's unrest.

The morning dawned windy and cold, with pine trees etched darkly against the golden fleece of sunrise clouds as Jade gathered Shaun and Holly and waited for the arrival of the mule train. Soon she heard the musical tinkle of bells and hooves clattering on the frozen trail. A young man riding a fine black Spanish mule came around some pine shrubs. Behind him he hauled a string of saddled mules and pack animals. Dave Wylet shouted to Berry, "The trail's full of ice further up. It took me an extra two hours."

Shaun's eyes widened at the sight of the mules and he surged toward them, anxious for adventure, but Holly's lips curled ruefully.

"Are we supposed to ride those creatures?"

Dave Wylet turned his head at the sound of her disdain. He wore a warm looking buffalo coat and hat, and the clear gray eyes peered at Holly and Jade as if seeing a mirage. Slowly he tipped his hat, and flashed a smile directed at Holly.

"Why, I don't believe it! Good morning, ladies! The name's Dave Wylet."

Jade glanced at Holly to see if she would answer and discovered that her sister's cranky mood was unexpectedly thawing. A pink flush tinted her cheeks, and for once in her life, Holly appeared speechless. Jade smiled to herself and deliberately kept silent.

"You ladies intending to ride with me to Carson?" Wylet asked, directing his question to Holly.

Jade nudged her when Holly seemed unable to reply.

"I—we're intending to ride to Carson, yes."

Wylet squinted and glanced around. "Where's your Pa?"

"In Virginia City."

He pushed his hat back and scanned her curiously. "What's his name?"

Holly hesitated and glanced sideways at Jade.

"Thomas O'Neil. My name is Jade, and this is my sister Holly O'Neil. We're from St. Louis. Do you—ah—know our father, Mr. Wylet?"

He flashed another grin. "No, ma'am, never heard of him."

"That's a relief," Holly murmured dryly to Jade.

"You were saying, Miss Holly?"

41

She cleared her throat. "Nothing, Mr. Wylet."

"I've heard of Samuel O'Neil. Any relation?"

"Yes, if he's a preacher," said Holly.

Wylet grinned. "Samuel's a preacher all right. A brave man to survive at Sun Mountain these fifteen years. He's not in Virginia town now, though. He's been up near the Badlands 'round Utah. Is he expecting you folks?"

"My sister Jade insists that he is," she quipped, but Jade ignored her. "We're friends of Roark Montgomery, so give me a tame mule."

"Montgomery! Why, I'll be! He's here?"

"He was. He went back down the mountain on business."

"He's after a badman," said Shaun in a voice laden with awe.

Wylet looked down at the boy with amusement. "A lot of 'em around," he said simply. "And who might you be?"

"Shaun O'Neil. This here's Keeper."

"A mighty fine cat, son. Better keep him tied, though, or you'll lose him over the pass."

"Oh, I keep him good and tied, sir!"

"Well, ladies, any friends of Montgomery deserve the best. How about this mule right here, Miss Holly? This is Lady Jane. Of course, you're twice the lady she is." He smiled and his eyes twinkled.

Holly grimaced. "Thank you, Mr. Wylet. Are you always so grand with your compliments?"

He smiled down at her. "Now, why don't you ride right next to me and Shaun, and I'll fill your ears all the way to Carson City."

"You're sure the mule won't get mad at me?"

"Lady Jane? Why, she owns the manners of Queen Victoria."

"Hey, Wylet!" Berry called. "Montgomery's rode in. Look's like you got yourself a lawman to ride with you."

At once Jade's heart pounded. He had come back. The reaction she felt to the news disturbed her, and she frowned to herself. *Don't be silly, Jade. He didn't come back because of you. He hardly knows you, and he thinks of you as a child. Besides, he's not only domineering, he's a bit conceited.*

But pausing, she stooped down and fumbled with her art satchel as if searching for something and, without turning her head, saw from the corner of her eye Roark Montgomery walking toward them.

"How are you, Roark?" Wylet called.

"Not bad, Dave. How's the trail further up?"

"This late in the season, ice and snow. I hear you're looking for a man. Maybe I've heard of him, what's his name?"

Silence followed, then Roark's voice dropped and Jade couldn't make out what he was saying. Had he deliberately lowered his voice? She glanced at them. A strange bubble of suspicion rose in her breast. It couldn't be her father; it just couldn't! Her green eyes riveted on Montgomery, but she could read nothing from his expression. His eyes came to hers, and quickly she lowered her gaze, busying herself with the art supplies.

A moment later he walked over to Holly who sat astride the mule and spoke quietly.

Jade buckled her satchel and tried not to listen to the snatches of conversation. She picked up only one

43

word. . .New York. Could Holly have told him about Aunt Norma?

"Good morning," came the smooth voice.

Jade glanced up. Roark stood a few feet away, the wind moving his dark jacket. The sight brought a quickening of her pulse.

She stood, hoping her expression was contained and mature. "Why, Mr. Montgomery, what a surprise. I expected you'd be in Placerville by now."

Roark scanned her. Did she detect a flicker of amusement at her feigned surprise?

"There was a change in plans."

She was reluctant to ask him directly about her father. After all, she could be wrong. She felt her way casually. "I take it the man you're looking for wasn't there?"

"No. I met a friend on the trail returning from Virginia City. He assured me the man is somewhere around Carson." He changed the subject. "I see you've survived your first night at Berry's Flat. You slept well?"

Jade caught the intended jest. So he was still set against her decision to go to Virginia City. And—he wasn't going to offer much information on the man he was seeking.

"Is this badman wanted for a train robbery?" she asked, mimicking Shaun's terminology.

"Train robbery?" His eyes came back to her, then glinted. He seemed to guess she was trying to keep the subject alive. He squinted up at the sky. Dark clouds were rolling with the wind. "Looks like snow. There's rough weather ahead if you go on with Wylet. The stage passes through here today on its way to Placerville. Don't you think you should go back?"

"Mr. Montgomery, I thought I made my intentions clear yesterday. I'm going to Virginia City." She stooped and picked up her satchel.

"You made your plans very clear, Miss O'Neil. I was hoping you'd reconsider after a good night's rest."

She smiled too sweetly. "I slept miserably, sir, but it will take more than a night in Strawberry to alter my decision to go on." She picked up her satchel and walked to the mule. *Just how was she supposed to mount the creature?*

Roark arched a brow. "Permit me," he offered smoothly, and held the mount steady. In a moment she was seated and refused to show any trepidation under his amused gaze.

"Ever ride a mule in St. Louis, Miss O'Neil?"

"No, but I'm up to riding one in Washoe, Mr. Montgomery."

She wanted to squirm as his gaze swept her. She guessed that her fatigue was not hidden from his eyes. If his father was a physician, as Holly had told her, Roark would know something about illness.

"Jade, are you sure you want to go through with this? Take my word for it, you need to be under a doctor's care."

The blunt statement brought a confused moment. She was prepared to resist, but the veiled sympathy in his gaze silenced a retort. She didn't know how to answer him. He wasn't going to be polite and let her pretend everything was normal.

"Holly had no right to tell you my private affairs," she said quietly.

"I'm glad she did. I know what you're trying to do now. I understand perfectly, as a matter of fact."

Beau crossed her mind. It was embarrassing to

realize that Roark knew that her fiance had broken their engagement.

"I know illness when I see it, and I strongly disagree with the risk you're taking."

"I've been well for a year. There's no reason to believe I'll become ill again."

"Isn't there?" he asked softly.

"No." But she felt the flush of her lie creep up her cheeks. She knew her attitude displeased the Lord. That very morning when she had washed her face she had noticed a faint darkness under her eyes and recognized it for what it was: the look of one who had been quite ill and still was.

"Being a pioneer missionary won't help you forget Beau Wilson."

"I didn't come here to impress Beau Wilson. At least allow me the credit to understand the difference between motives for service that honor God and those that are self-seeking."

"My dear, I wasn't questioning your devotion. The truth is, for such a frail young thing, I find your courage commendable."

Frail young thing!

"There are many ways to serve God without deliberately risking your life."

"Do you always lecture women like some overbearing guardian, Mr. Montgomery?"

He smiled, undisturbed, his voice still smooth, "Granted, you're a determined young lady who finds a contrary opinion irksome. But in this instance, Miss O'Neil, I think you do need a guardian. If you force yourself to go on like this, you could end up fainting in your saddle and that could be dangerous. Let me tell you something about pack mules. They

46

don't stop for anybody. They press ahead and without pity for anything that gets in their way."

"I'm sure you would know more about mules than I do," she said firmly, "but I've told you. I am my own guardian. And—I'm not about to faint."

The silence hemmed them in. His eyes grew slate-colored. He pulled his hat lower and scanned her.

"You know," he breathed, "you've got a stubborn streak a mile wide."

Surprised, she turned to study his expression. It was Holly she considered to be the stubborn one in the family. Jade half expected to find the hint of Roark's usual amusement. It wasn't there. His jaw was set.

"I'm learning a few things about you, too, Roark Montgomery. You're a very domineering man. You think a woman should give in every time you order her about."

He laughed his dismissal, but his eyes showed subdued challenge. "And you're the little girl who isn't about to give an inch, is that it?"

Jade snatched the reins from his hand. "I believe I told you before that I am not a child." And not waiting for an answer, she dragged her eyes from his and stared straight ahead to show the conversation was ended.

Roark's mouth curved, and he tipped his hat. "As you wish. Good day, Miss O'Neil." He turned and walked away.

Dave Wylet was by the mules, tightening cinches as Roark walked up. He followed Roark's gaze.

"Nice. How'd she escape the veranda of a Southern mansion?"

"You tell me. She has a mind of her own, though.

There's iron under that silken exterior."

"What's she planning for Virginia City?"

Roark looked at him with a slanted brow. "To convert Winnemucca," he said wryly.

Wylet almost choked. "Chief of the Piutes?! Say, now," Wylet breathed, with a twinkle in his eyes. "Looks to me, Roark, like you got your hands full this time."

Chapter 4

As evening approached and the mules pressed toward the summit, the weather turned colder rapidly. Snow blanketed the forest floor and the wind had picked up, bringing in whitish-gray clouds that heralded a storm.

The mules seemed to feel the warning in the brisk wind, Jade thought. Instinctively they hurried forward, knowing the trail so well that she simply gave hers the reins. After riding along hour after hour, she had become aware of little but extreme weariness and struggled to keep her teeth from chattering. At last, though, Dave Wylet rode up into the trees, and, a few minutes later, he stopped in a clearing.

Jade sat wearily on the mule, her eyes resting on a large emerald-sapphire lake.

"Lake Tahoe," called Wylet. "Pretty, isn't she? The

Jewel-Lady, I call her. We'll camp here for the night."

Jade was too tired to make a comment, and almost too stiff and sore to dismount. She expected to hear Holly complaining, but, surprisingly, she was in a bright mood. Jade forced herself to help find dry branches and pine cones, but all she could think of was lying down where it was warm and falling asleep. Her feet were like cold lead as she carried pine boughs and grass to make her bed for the night.

Later, the fragrant smell of smoke from the campfire hung heavily in the air as Roark read the Scriptures aloud. The words seemed to bring a spark of warmth and life to the cold darkness. Jade felt a comforting sense of God's nearness as her eyes grew heavy. Soon Roark's voice became distant and she was tired, very tired. . . .

A small hand gripped her shoulder and shook it anxiously. "Jade! Jade!" Shaun whispered. "Wake up!"

Her mind didn't want to work. She raised herself to her elbow. The camp was dark and quiet; she didn't see anyone but Shaun, whose eyes were wide and frightened. He was struggling to keep his lip from quivering.

All remnants of sleep fled. "What is it, honey?"

"I—I can't find Keeper."

"What? Shaun, didn't you tie him to a tree?"

"I thought I tied him good," he quavered, "but something must've scared him, because he got his head out from under the collar." A sudden splash of tear ran down his cheek, and he wiped it quickly away.

Jade gave him a hug. "We'll find him," she whispered, and threw off her blanket.

50

"I know he's up there, Jade." He pointed toward the cluster of trees. "I think he's caught on a shrub. If we don't find him before morning, it'll be too late. Mr. Wylet says the snow's coming. Keeper will freeze, or a bear—"

"What is it now?" moaned Holly, poking her head up from under the blanket.

"Keeper's missing. Get up and help me look for him."

Holly groaned again as she tried to turn over. "Oooh—every muscle in my body hurts. An entire day on a mule! And you want me to get up in the cold? And look—it's starting to rain!"

"Then I'll look. Go back to sleep." Jade moved away into the darkness with Shaun. The clouds were heavy, and strong gusts of wind whined through the branches.

"We'll go uphill. But keep the campfire in sight, Shaun. We won't get lost that way."

Shaun's look of desperation reinforced what Jade already knew. If anything happened to that cat, it would be a serious emotional loss, a loss her little brother might not be able to handle. Ignoring her weariness, she grabbed his arm and started with him toward an incline of Ponderosa pine.

"He went this way, Jade! I'm sure of it."

A few drops of rain were falling as they moved through the pine shrubs. Shaun was pulling her. "Hurry, Jade!"

Ahead in the darkness was a steep embankment. Shaun dropped her hand and surged ahead. "I think I saw him, Jade!"

"Careful, Shaun! It's too dark to see anything."

"He's up here, I just heard him!"

"You'll frighten him. Move slowly. Call him."

"Keeper? Here, Keeper!'

With the wind rushing through the trees, Jade wondered how he could hear anything. She paused to listen. Shaun's voice echoed to her, now coming from further away. Suddenly she remembered. Roark had mentioned a cliff! "No, Wait!"

Jade scrambled up the embankment, feeling the soft earth give way in a little avalanche beneath her feet. She grabbed the pine brush to help pull herself up. *Lord, please protect him.* The words repeated themselves like a drumbeat within her heart. Protect. Protect. . . .But her body's frailty demanded its toll. Short of breath, her heart pounding from exertion, she struggled up the hill as though she had been running for a mile. The wind caught her hood and blew it back from her head. Its cold fingers sent her hair tumbling from the pins that had held it up. He lungs were burning when she reached the top of the embankment; the high altitude left her gasping for air.

"Shaun!" The wind hurled her voice back into her face. She moved forward, her feet stumbling over stones unseen in the darkness. Ahead, she heard Shaun's shout, but she stopped, uncertain which way to go.

"Keeper!" His voice was distant now. "Keeper, where are you? I didn't mean to get mad at you tonight. Nice kitty, where are you, Keeper? Here, kitty, here kitty—"

Jade strained to see in the dark. The incline continued another sixty feet or more among the thick silhouettes of tall pine. She turned and looked back over her shoulder. "Stay within sight of the campfire," she had told him. But had he? A faint reddish glow could be seen among the trees. She cupped her hands to her mouth. "Shaun, come back. Do you hear me?"

Nothing sounded but the wind, and the drops of rain were changing to snow. She suspected that the incline was a good ten feet higher, yet in the dark it was difficult to tell. Jade forced herself to renew her careful climb upward. Then his distant cry reached her ears.

"Jade! I found him!"

No sooner did a sigh of relief reach her lips than Shaun shouted, terror in his voice, "Jade!"

She struggled upward, the soil slipping out from beneath her heet. Her fingers clutched at protruding rocks. Her body couldn't keep up with her will. The reality of her weakness, and the fear of failure, set in. "Lord, help me find him! Please!"

There came a distant, sullen rumble of thunder. A zigzag of intense white lightning lit up the eastern sky and momentarily outlined dark pine trees and boulders.

"Over here, Jade!"

This time she could pinpoint the sound. She was gasping when she reached Shaun and found him clinging to a pine shrub protruding from the side of the mountain. Keeper was in one arm, his other hand held tenaciously to a branch. *Thank you, Father!* The prayer rushed through her, carried on the flood of her relief.

"Hold on, I'll have you up in a minute. . . ."

"Hurry Jade—"

She could feel the loosened pebbles and earth breaking up beneath her elbow and chest, as she laid down on the edge of the cliff, straining to reach his arm. Fearing a wash-out of mud and rock and a terrifying slide down into darkness, she fought to pull Shaun up slowly. Every inch gained was a victory that encouraged Jade to try harder. At last he was up high enough to crawl, and in another moment Shaun was safely clutched within her embrace. "Oh, Father, thank you. . . ."

Jade felt a rush of joy. "We made it, Shaun," she gasped.

Shaun's arm fastened around her neck, and with the other, he held Keeper close to his heart. The wind was roaring through the tree branches now and snow was falling heavily, but to Jade, the moment was as sweet as the warm breath of a summer breeze.

Then, through a sudden lull, she heard someone shouting her name. "Jade! Where are you?"

"Up here," she called, and not even the weakness in her voice cooled her satisfaction. "We're all right."

In a moment, Roark appeared with Dave Wylet and Holly. Jade struggled to her feet.

"I—I fell trying to reach Keeper," Shaun explained. "He was clinging to the shrub and—"

"What!" cried Holly. "You slipped over the cliff? Shaun! You might have fallen to your death! And for a cat!"

"I would have, Holly, but Jade got here in time. She pulled me up! And Keeper!"

"Shaun, that cat has been nothing but trouble since we left St. Louis!"

Shaun's expression crumbled, and he held Keeper even tighter.

"Leave him alone, Holly," said Jade.

"Jade, you're not hurt?" asked Roark.

"No, I'm fine, just a little tired that's all. We did well enough, didn't we, Shaun?"

54

Shaun wordlessly threw an arm around her waist, and Jade held him, exhausted, but still pleased.

"We better get back to camp," Wylet said softly.

"I—I think Keeper has a scratch on his foot," Shaun said haltingly.

"We'll take a look at him when we get back to camp. C'mon, son."

When Wylet had led Holly and Shaun back down the slope, Roark's silhouette drew closer to her. She couldn't read his expression.

"You took a risk in coming alone, Jade. Why didn't you come to me before you left with Shaun? You knew I'd help. All you had to do was ask me."

"There wasn't enough time. Shaun was in a panic to find the cat."

"You might have fallen yourself. You're not strong enough."

"But I didn't fall," she said, unable to mask her jubilation. "Nor did I fail."

"No, you didn't fail. You saved Shaun's life. You're a courageous young girl. But then, you wouldn't have failed by coming to me for help, either."

The wind struck with a bitter blast. Exhaustion was setting in and Jade shuddered, drawing her soiled cloak about her. It was ruined. She would never get it clean again.

"Jade, you're not listening."

She looked up at him, seeing little but his silhouette.

"What are you afraid of? Certainly not risk. Is it the fear of limitation and physical weakness, of needing others? Is that why you insist on independence?"

"Please, I don't know what you mean. We better get back. Look, the snow is coming down harder."

He took hold of her arm. "It's Beau, isn't it?"

"No, not anymore."

"Did the broken engagement hurt so much?"

"He and the mission board might as well have told me I was worthless because I was ill. They were wrong."

"If that's what they intended, of course they were wrong. But why do you need to prove it to yourself? Don't you know how precious you are to God?"

Precious to God. . .was she? Of course. . .she knew that, and yet. . . .

"I—I think we should go back."

"You should be happy to be rid of Beau."

She caught her breath. "Whatever do you—"

"Should I tell you my opinion of a man who'd break an engagement by letting his daddy do it for him?"

Jade was glad that darkness hid them. "I suppose you'd handle it quite differently."

"To begin with, I wouldn't find myself in that position. If I wanted a woman enough to marry her, illness wouldn't change my mind. And if something did come up to prove the engagement to be wrong, I'd handle it myself. So you see," he said lightly, "if I were you, I wouldn't shed any more tears over this Beau."

"I don't intend to shed any more tears over any man, thank you. I've learned my lesson about them. I'm going to Virginia City to pursue my art sketches and to labor among the Piutes."

"I'm delighted that you've managed to get your love life all in order, Miss O'Neil. I'm sure matters are tidied up quite nicely, and your emotions are garrisoned from any further attack."

Stung, Jade turned abruptly to make her own way

back down the slope. She took several steps only to discover that her knees wanted to buckle and almost lost her balance. Roark caught her elbow, keeping her from falling.

"I'll carry you."

"I don't need to be carried."

Ignoring her protests, he swept her up into his strong embrace. Her cheek rested against his leather jacket as he carried her back toward camp, and she fought to hold her feelings in check. He must not know how comforting this felt.

"*Please,* put me down."

"You may not think so now, my dear, but your noble trek has weakened you, possibly even to the point of a relapse. Tuberculosis demands lots of bedrest and good meals."

At the word tuberculosis, Jade shrank within like a snail into its shell. She hated the word, and she hated even more for him to speak it in regard to her. Unfortunately, weakness began to demand that she sleep.

"You sound like a doctor," she murmured.

"I've always had a secondary interest in medicine. In fact, I attended medical school for a time."

"You! When did you become a lawman?"

"Oh. . .three years ago."

"What made you leave medical school to wear a gun?"

"A deep dark secret," he said lightly. "One that I've no intention of sharing with you, at least not now."

"I think I've guessed all ready."

There was a moment of silence. "Oh?"

"Yes," she murmured wearily, allowing herself the pleasure of leaving her palm resting against his jacket.

"You fell madly in love with the daughter of the president of the medical school. . .and she rejected you."

He laughed. "He didn't have a daughter."

"Then a San Francisco socialite."

"I don't fall in love so easily."

She stiffened and came wide awake. Frowning, she tried to judge the tone of his voice. Was he implying that she did? Had he been teasing? She imagined an amused glint of toleration in his smile, and the idea made her mute. Roark Montgomery had made it clear that she was no more than a child to him. At the moment, Jade felt anything but that.

Chapter 5

The snow had quit falling two days ago, leaving yesterday wild with winds that Dave Wylet called diabolis or devil winds. When Jade rode up Gold Canyon toward Sun Mountain, however, the winds had eased. The Nevada sky was a brazen blue, like polished slate, and the Washoe mountain range stood etched against the horizon in artistic shades of purple and black.

The beauty startled Jade who rode beside Roark with Shaun and Holly, and she viewed her surroundings through the eyes of her art paints and brushes. Wild, harsh, majestic, untouched by the littleness of man, the mountains stood as a monument to the greatness of their Creator. How strong the granite fortresses, she thought, and how her frailty was intensified when compared with such silent strength.

At the mouth of Gold Canyon, they rode through a narrow rocky pass between two great rocks. "Devil's

Gate, they call it," Roark said.

Shaun breathlessly read the sign stretching across the narrow dirt path. "Devil's Gate Toll Road - 50¢ - Pass on and up."

"We're almost there. There's a hotel in Gold Hill. We'll stop at it," Roark told Jade.

Gold Hill. The words conjured up visions of rich, yellow splendor in Jade's mind, but there were no gold streets, nor any golden hills gleaming in the late afternoon sunlight when they finally arrived.

"This—is Gold Hill?"

"It is, my dear Miss O'Neil." Roark's eyes glinted as he swung her down from the saddle. "Welcome to Washoe."

Holly sat astride the mule looking glum, refusing to get down. The sparkle had left her eyes. "We should have stayed in Carson City like Dave—I mean, Mr. Wylet asked us."

Jade blurted, "Where's the town?"

Roark kept a straight face. "You're looking at it."

"Where?"

"There."

She stood, staring off at some—cabins? Huts? the soiled lean-tos were made of canvas; a few were made of board, but the rest were mere blankets and shirts flapping in the wind.

At least there was a hotel like Roark had told her. The name above the entrance read Vesy. Jade's eyes swept the two adjoining sections. One was a three story wooden structure, the other a two story building constructed of rubble stone with a covered wooden walk. She heard piano music drifting out. The gambling fever was burning even at this hour; men were playing Monte when they entered the hotel lobby.

"I'll get you settled here, then see what I can learn about Samuel."

How Roark ended up getting them a room of their own, she wasn't sure. She only knew that without him they would never have made it this far. Surely the Lord had sent Roark Montgomery. Jade smiled to herself. He must never know that she considered him her "guardian angel," not after all the fuss she had put up to maintain her independence.

The room he escorted them to had a double bed, a trundle, and a dresser with a mirror.

"Oooh, it's gorgeous," cried Holly. "And a bath! Hey—Shaun! I'm first! Get that cat out of the tub!"

Jade's brows came together. How would she ever pay him back? Already she owed him for their meals, the cost of the mules from Strawberry to Virginia City, and now the hotel room.

She glanced at him sideways. "I'll pay you back as soon as I sell some of my sketches."

"I told you once I don't collect debts from beautiful young women."

The idea that he found her so, and said it even though spoken lightly, brought its moment of pleasure, but she affected indifference. "Thank you, but I always pay my debts, Mr. Montgomery."

"Then I shall change my mind. One day I will see you pay in full."

He drew her aside into the hall, saying quietly, "I've been assured the owner will keep an eye on you. But I want you to promise me you'll stay out of trouble until Samuel gets here."

"Why, Mr. Montgomery," she said innocently, "what possible trouble could I get into here?"

His dark brows slanted. "No comment. Take your

61

meals up here. Have you any idea where Samuel is?"

"He has a dugout in Sun Mountain, but my father owns a claim out at Seven-Mile Canyon. We're intending to go there and move into his cabin with him."

"Jade, this is no time to play games with me. I want the truth. Is your father expecting you?"

"Well. . .I wrote him, but he never answered. . . . Samuel doesn't know either."

"So little sister Holly was right. I could lecture you on the errors of your ways, but I'll spare you this time."

"How generous of you, sir."

"Now, tell me this, do you know if your father has ever gone by another name?"

Jade was embarrassed to admit it. She felt his eyes measure her response. "Well—that is—" She stopped.

"Yes?"

"Why do you want to know?" she asked cautiously.

"Any information will make it easier to locate him."

She stared up at him. A small war of conflicting emotions battled within her heart. Finally, she replied, "As a matter of fact, he did use another name. Before my mother died he wrote her a letter from Virginia City."

"Do you still have the letter?"

"It's in my bag."

When she lifted her gaze, she saw a flicker of uncertainty in his eyes. She was sure he was debating something in his mind that was bothering him.

"I'll need that letter, Jade."

Her eyes fell to the badge just showing beneath his jacket. She crossed the room and opened her bag.

Roark leaned his shoulder against the door, watching her. When she turned to him, she paused at the sweeping glance he gave her. In that moment, it seemed as if he had hoped she wouldn't find it. Slowly she crossed the room and handed him the worn envelope.

"Jack Dawson," he read.

"I don't know why he chose that name, but he does gamble," she confessed. "My mother told me he had a terrible temper, and was—well—rather fast with a gun."

When Roark remained silent, she hastened, "I told you, my father is not a Christian."

"I'll return this to Samuel," and he started to turn down the hall. Jade followed him, somewhat baffled. Was that all he was going to say?

"How long will you be gone?"

His eyes became remote. "I'm not sure, yet."

Jade searched his face, but it had become as blank as a granite wall. Was it a veiled hint that he wasn't intending to come back, but didn't care to say so?

He paused to look down at her. A heady feeling enveloped her when he raised his hand to hold her chin lightly. "Remember, stay out of trouble," he said again. His hand dropped. He disappeared down the stairs.

Jade reentered the room and crossed to the window overlooking the street. Her stomach felt as if she had swallowed lead. A few minutes later she watched him ride off in the direction of Sun Mountain.

Boom towns, like Jonah's gourd, came up in a night

63

and perished in a night. By the summer of 1860 more than 10,000 people had sprawled beneath Sun Mountain. When Roark Montgomery had ridden into Virginia City, he was not surprised that out of the silver bonanza, a full-grown "city" had emerged, bypassing the stage of its infancy.

Wherever he looked he saw men digging or throwing together a building. For every hut there seemed a dozen gambling saloons. He left the hotel and walked into the Bucket of Blood.

"What'll you have?" the man behind the counter asked.

"Coffee."

The man's eyes shot over him, but he poured hot liquid into a tin cup and set it down. The brew looked like mud. It tasted almost as bad.

"Ever heard of Jack Dawson?" Roark asked.

"He ain't been around for a spell. Dawson must be a popular fellow. You ain't the only one lookin' for him." He gestured with his head to a table across the room. "So's Ramos."

Roark turned. A lean man with shoulder length yellow hair and a drooping mustache was watching him. As Roark's gaze met his, he stood and sauntered up to the counter.

"I aim to find him first, Montgomery. And when I do, his next address will be Boot Hill."

Roark stared, trying to place Ramos. "Do I know you?"

"Name's Bill Ramos. News is out you're here to arrest Dawson."

Roark thought of his meeting with Jesse and Ernie at Strawberry. They must have come to Virginia City looking for Thomas O'Neil. He wasn't surprised. That meant Thomas knew he was here, too.

"News of a lawman coming in travels like a prairie fire, Montgomery. Half the men in the Comstock are wanted somewhere. I'm clean, but I intend to finish Dawson. Anyone who gets in my way has only himself to blame."

"I'll give you a warning, Ramos. Stay out of my way, or I'll be bringing two men back. I don't know why you want him, but I'll handle Dawson."

"He stole my claim out at Seven-Mile. My brother Ronnie, and me, we struck some good diggin's. Rich ore. We took some in to have it checked at Nevada City. While we were gone, he shot our partner in the back and tore the page out of the ledger book showing we were the owners."

"Stay out of it. If you're telling the truth about the claim, I'll see that you get it back. Interfere, and you'll end up buried with him on Boot Hill."

Ramos' black eyes glittered. "Like I said, Montgomery. I aim to find him first." Turning, he walked out, each step deliberate and loud.

Roark turned to the man behind the counter. "Where can I find the preacher, Samuel O'Neil?"

"He's got a place in the Mountain. Ask around, you'll find him. He's been gone for a week—least I've missed his preachin' at me. Been nice havin' him out of my conscience."

Roark smiled. "I'll tell him to keep up the good work."

"He doesn't need encouragement."

"Samuel's back." A slow Arkansas drawl spoke up from the end of the counter. "He rode in last night with an arrow in him."

"Wretched Piutes," said another.

65

"Trouble?" Roark asked.

"The Injuns claim we're ruining Washoe by chopping down all the pinon pine for burning and building."

"They need the cones for food in the winter," offered the lanky man from Arkansas.

"If they come, we'll be ready," said the bartender. "Ain't no Indians chasin' us out of Virginia town, not with a silver bonanza in the workin'."

Roark finished his coffee in silence, then left. He walked his horse to the slope of Sun Mountain. The sun was falling behind it, casting shadows across the rocky soil. Virginia City was sprawled on the lap of the Mountain. Dismounting, he walked uphill to where some men were starting a shaft. They had dug about six feet or so. He watched them from under his hat until a redhead squinted up at him.

"What do you think?" asked Roark.

"Too soon to tell. It don't look like Sutter's to me." He pulled up his soiled trousers and spat. "Why, in '49 in California we was pickin' up gold nuggets."

"Seen Samuel O'Neil?"

He pointed farther up. "He's got himself a regular church inside the Mountain."

"Inside?"

"Go have a see. He's there. Nursin' a wound."

Roark soon found Samuel's dugout and called out a greeting.

Abruptly, a rugged, broad shouldered man appeared, wearing a worn black frock reaching to his knees. Heavy boots covered his muscled calves.

"I saw you coming," said Samuel O'Neil. "Who be you, lad?"

"Roark Montgomery." He showed his badge. "From San Francisco."

"A lawman, huh?" The dark eyes gleamed and measured Roark. "Is that so? Well, that's better than most around here. Even so, you aiming to reach heaven by showing Him your badge?"

Roark hesitated. So. . .this was Samuel. He smiled slightly. "I don't think He would be impressed. Besides being a lawman, I also carry this Book."

A smile spread across Samuel's bronzed face when his eyes fell on the small Bible. "Now you're talking my language, lad. Come in. Come in. Don't just stand there!"

Samuel still bore a handsomeness for his fifty odd years. The eyes were set far apart below bushy arched brows that were as black as a raven. His thin hawk nose flared into wide nostrils over a flowing mustache which drooped downward and disappeared into his short beard.

Roark saw little resemblance to Jade, but knowing she had an uncle like Samuel O'Neil was a consolation. If anyone could curtail her risky ambitions, it was Samuel.

Roark's eyes fell to Samuel's arm; it was in a sling. "Piutes?"

Samuel's brows came together, and he winced as he reached to touch his shoulder. "So that's what they're saying! Blame everything on them Piutes. No, it's a bullet wound. Rascal's still in there, too."

At once Roark was alert. "Who shot you?"

"It was dark. Somebody after my brother Tommy."

Roark thought of the Ramos brothers. If he didn't find Thomas O'Neil soon, he wouldn't live to stand trial in San Francisco. "You better let me get that bullet out."

"Obliged if you would, lad. I got some water boiling

now." He reached over and produced a knife. "Make it quick. I got no time to be held up in here. I've got to cross the Humboldt River."

"Looking for your brother Thomas, or the man who put the bullet in you?"

Samuel squinted up at him. "Say you're a lawman?"

Roark knew he must be honest with Samuel. "I'm here to arrest a man, but I'm not looking forward to it. It's keeping me awake at nights."

Samuel grimaced but made no sound as Roark worked. "I'm suspecting the worst of news, lad. Go ahead. I'm listening."

"I've come for Thomas O'Neil, alias Jack Dawson."

"So. . ." sighed Samuel.

"He's wanted for the death of two men and the wounding of a third. The shooting took place several years ago on board the *Sutter Steamer*, a riverboat on the San Francisco Bay. The card dealer is dead. So is the captain."

Samuel sighed. "Tommy's got a bad temper, that's no lie, always has—since we were boys. What about the fella who was wounded? Ouch!—Easy, lad!"

"His right arm is crippled. He's a physician who can no longer perform surgery. He's Dr. James Montgomery, my father."

"Ah. . ."

After a muffled groan from Samuel, Roark held up the bullet. "What do you have to pour on the wound?"

Samuel focused his burning eyes. "That tarantula juice isn't permitted in my abode. Not even for medical purposes. Seen it kill and maim too many miserable souls. Use water, lad."

"Water won't do."

"You sound like a doctor yourself. Had any training?"

"Some. Water won't do," He said again.

"This kind will," Samuel said dryly. "It's enough to make a man sick. It comes from the mountain and has arsenic in it. Mule died the other day. . .poor critter drank too much." He shook his head. "Be sure you go easy on it yourself. . . . About Thomas, he shot your father?"

"A stray bullet."

Samuel's dark eyes probed his soul. "Any root of bitterness, lad?"

Roark met his piercing eyes evenly. His voice was calm. "Not anymore. For the last year I've been free of that poison. It took awhile."

"I'm pleased to hear that. No personal quest for vengeance?"

"I believe that the wisdom of God is behind the so-called accidents of life. It helps to know there's a purpose in the bitter cup. Retribution is best left to God."

"Humph. . ." Samuel's eyes narrowed as he took in the rugged young man, measuring his character as well as his strength. "You're a refreshing drink of cold water, Roark Montgomery. I believe you. So I'll risk telling you more about Tommy—alias Jack Dawson.

"Tommy was the youngest of five boys. The rest of us are scattered here and there, and sadly, never keep in touch. The others yell loudly enough at believing in Christ, but only He knows. I surely don't. They want nothing to do with me.

"Tommy, however, is another story. He's never claimed faith. He's addicted to gambling, shoots fast, too. Whenever he needs money or is in trouble, he comes to me. I preach and he listens. That's as far as it goes. When I'm done, he goes right back to his cards.

"I've always loved Tommy. Somehow, in spite of his badness, he meant the most to me. I've spent more time on my face before God for him than all the others put together. And still he's as wrong as can be!

"He cares nothing for his kids, and you've never seen a finer lot, especially my lovely Jade and Shaun."

"Jade's at Vesy's Hotel in Gold Hill."

Samuel drew in a breath and stood to his feet. "Jade? Here? This is no place for her!"

"You'll have a hard time convincing her of that. She's got some of your missionary spirit. Having met you, I now know where it came from." Roark smiled. "She's determined to work with you to teach the Scriptures. Jade's also a very ill young woman. You knew that?"

Samuel groaned. "The relapse came then? I've been praying night and day it wouldn't."

"I haven't said anything to her yet, but I'd like her to go to San Francisco to visit my father. He's the best physician around."

"She'll go to 'Frisco all right. I'll insist upon it. I'll go to Gold Hill tonight."

Roark's eyes were troubled, but his jaw was set with disciplined resolve as he spoke. "Samuel, first of all, I'm a lawman. Regardless of my concern for Jade's health, I'm sworn to uphold my badge. I'm under orders from the California governor to bring Thomas in to stand trial."

Samuel sank to the horsechair cushion. "I can understand your dilemma, lad. Does Jade know you've come to arrest her father?"

"No. I wanted to see her here safely, first. I think it would be best for you to break the news."

"The truth is, you just missed Tommy. There's been trouble over a claim at Seven-Mile that Tommy says is his. He's brought in three men from Salt Lake to back him up. But after the bullets flew last night, he and his friends took off."

"I've met Bill Ramos. He insists Thomas jumped the claim."

Samuel rubbed his beard. "Ramos may have something there. At one time Tommy worked with the Ramos brothers out at Seven-Mile. Something came up between them and turned them into enemies."

"Ramos seemed to think Thomas shot his partner while he and his brother were in Nevada City having the ore sampled."

"I hate to admit it, but it sounds reasonable. As to who owns the feet of lode, it's hard to say. There're so many claims on the Mountain now that they overlap three and four deep, and there's confusion in the recorder's office. Tommy denies it, of course. But then, he has a way of looking a man straight in the eye and lying. Anyway, I talked him into riding to Carson with me to talk to a lawyer named Stewert."

"Bill Stewert from San Francisco?"

"That's the fella. You know him?"

"He's an acquaintance of my father. He's a good lawyer. The best."

"We got waylaid between Gold Hill and Carson. That's where I picked up this bullet. It was meant for Tommy."

"The Ramos brothers?"

71

"Truth is, I don't know, lad. They're plenty riled with Tommy."

"You've no idea where he might have gone?"

Samuel shook his head. "He's got three men with him. One was named Letterman. Another was Jesse, I think."

"I need to find him before Ramos does."

"Tommy will show himself. I've something he wants." Samuel reached into his pocket and pulled out a folded paper. "With those bullets flying last night, he wasn't sure if he'd make it this time. He told me to keep this for him. You better have a see."

Roark saw names, dates, and locations of claims written in pencil. Some had been erased, and other names written in, including the name Thomas O'Neil. "It's been torn from a mining ledger."

"The miners just went into the saloon where Nick kept the ledger book and signed their names in pencil. Not very smart, but until the silver rush, there wasn't much trouble in Washoe."

"The ledger wasn't protected?"

"Anyone could walk in and make whatever amends he wanted. Looks like Tommy did."

"So they settle disputes with guns. And the fastest draw wins."

"Afraid so, lad."

"If the Ramos brothers find out you have this, they'll kill you to get it. I'd like to hold onto it."

Samuel got to his feet, still holding his shoulder. "It's better off with you than me. Bill Stewert says more land is claimed than Washoe can provide! Says Washoe's in a mess. Arbitration is the thing."

"I think he's right. He's going to have his hands full. I think we all will."

Roark walked back to the opening of the dugout, and Samuel followed him. "I want to take a look at that mine out at Seven-Mile. If there's a cabin, I'd like to put up there for a few weeks."

"Go right ahead, lad. No need to warn you to be careful."

"Samuel. . .I don't want Jade near the mine."

"I'll ride out to the hotel and talk to her tonight. Any message, lad?"

Roark's expression was inscrutable. "No. I've no choice but to arrest her father. There's not much I can say to her."

When Samuel arrived at the Vesy Hotel, Jade immediately recognized him—and knew by his expression that he had bad news. After the round of hugs and words of welcome, Samuel insisted that she have a cup of coffee with him downstairs in the Great Room.

"What about me, Uncle Samuel, can I go, too?" cried Shaun.

Samuel grabbed him and tossed him into the air, smiling at his nephew's squeal. He caught him as he came down, pretending he lost his grip, and Shaun squealed again.

"Now that I got you, lad, do you think I'm going to let you get away from me again? You stay and look after Keeper until we get back. Then I'll take you down for a sarsaparilla."

Winking at the boy, he took Jade by the arm and went downstairs. Seated in the dining room with Uncle Samuel, Jade stared into the rugged, bearded face, and for a moment, she couldn't speak. Finally she broke the silence. "Roark came to arrest my father."

Samuel's voice was quiet. "I'm afraid he has, lass. When a man wears a badge, he has his duty."

With a sinking feeling of finality, Jade realized that Roark had known all along what he would do, yet he had kept it from her. And all the while pretending to care about them. She had even given him the letter using the name Jack Dawson.

"He wants you to go to San Francisco to see his father, Dr. James Montgomery, lass, and I'm in total agreement."

"Go with him? Does Roark Montgomery think I would ever trust him again?" Her voice shook, and her hands were trembling. "He lied to me."

"Lass, never call a man like Montgomery a liar."

"Then what do you call his deliberate deceit?"

Samuel's gaze riveted on Jade. "He didn't deceive you purposely. I'm a good judge of character, and I can see he's got plenty of it. If he didn't mention your Pa's trouble with the San Francisco law, it was because he cared too much to add more burden to your shoulders. He came straight to me—just as he should have."

"He should have been honest with *me*," she fumed. "Now I know why he went out of his way to show us *kindness*. And this room! I won't stay here another moment while he pays my bills! San Francisco is out of the question. Pa's got a cabin out at Seven-Mile, and I'm going there."

"You're making a mistake, lass."

"And I'll pay him back every penny he's spent on us. Somehow I'll sell my paintings, and when my father turns up, I'll believe him innocent until I have good reason not to."

"Now you listen to me, Jade. I know Thomas far better than you. When was the last time you saw him?

Why, you must've been in pigtails. I've a lifetime of experience with Tommy."

Jade was ashamed to admit she hadn't seen him in over six years. She also knew he had taken advantage of her mother and denied her the support of a husband and provider.

"He's still my father!" she said, swallowing back the pain in her throat. "He wouldn't kill."

"He was drunk on whiskey when he pulled his gun. A man who wouldn't harm when he was sober does careless things when his brain is fuzzy."

"I know all that! I'm not making excuses, Uncle Samuel. Pa might do many things that are wrong—but shoot two men on a riverboat? I can't believe it."

Samuel gazed intently into her face. "Saying this is as painful to me as it is to you. He's my brother. My little brother, and he's always been that to me. Jade, I've seen Tommy come close to drawing his gun on a man over a card game a dozen times."

Jade winced with pain. This was not the way she remembered her father. She felt ill and pushed the cup of coffee aside. How could it have come to this? And now. . . ?

Chapter 6

Jade and Holly left Samuel's dugout in Sun Mountain and walked to where he kept his mule. Maybe she could get Toby to saddle the creature for her.

"But, Jade! You could get lost going out to Seven-Mile Canyon," Holly protested.

"I sketched the location of the mine from a drawing I found in Samuel's desk. Look, Holly, we've a right to Pa's cabin. We can't stay here with Samuel all winter. We've been here a week already. Besides, if Pa shows up at Seven-Mile I intend to be there to see him."

"I hope you know what you're doing, Jade. You heard Samuel say it was dangerous to ride out there with those Ramos brothers poking around."

"I intend to find out what they're searching for. Don't worry so, I'll be careful."

Holly wrinkled her brow. "Maybe I should go with you—"

"You better stay with Shaun. Samuel won't be back from his trip to the Humboldt River until Friday."

"Are you sure it isn't Roark Montgomery you're intending to find?"

"No," Jade said flatly. "I haven't seen him since he brought us to the hotel in Gold Hill, and I don't care if I ever see him again. He's looking for Pa. I doubt if he's anywhere near the cabin."

"But what if he is? Samuel seemed to think he was going to stay there until Pa showed up."

"Then he'll need to find some other place to lay his trap for Pa. I intend to move in as soon as Samuel returns."

They both turned as the old, grizzled miner named Toby came up. "Howdy do, ladies."

Jade cast him a smile. "Toby, you're just the man I wanted to see. Would you mind showing me how to saddle one of these creatures?"

"Why, there ain't nuthin' to it, Miss Jade." He took the saddle from the peg. "Where ya headed, girl?"

"Seven-Mile. I'm an artist. I'm going to spend the day doing some sketching out there."

"The weather ain't so good fer sittin' out in. You be careful now. There's plenty of mines and dry holes out there. Along the base of the Mountain you'll find William's Station, Steamboat, Dutch Nick's, and Sutro's holdings." He pushed his soiled hat back and scratched his gray locks. "You be sure to let everyone know you're ol' Samuel's niece. They all know the Preacher."

"Thanks, Toby, I will. There's a stew on the hearth for lunch. Holly will get you a bowl."

"Won't mind if'n I do," he said with a toothless grin.

The morning was gray with clouds as Jade rode toward the canyon. Those who knew Washoe were claiming that it was going to be a bad winter. Dave Wylet had warned them when he came down the day before from Carson to visit Holly that the snows had come early to the Sierras. All who could were thinking about leaving until spring.

The mule's hooves clattered across the rocks, and the wind howled down the canyon. The boulders lifted steeply in some places, and there was the pungent odor of sage. Thousands of trampling hooves had made the soil thin and powdery, and the dust swirled up ahead and played itself out in the silence.

Jade followed her sketch of the map carefully until finally she saw a stone hut. She climbed down from the mule and tied him to a shrub. The cabin sat in a natural amphitheater in the hills with a spring of water nearby and, not far off, what looked to her like a prospect hole. As she walked toward it, she saw some reddish rocks and others with a bluish cast to them. Recognizing it from the miners' talk, this had to be the "blue stuff," the ore that was rich with silver.

As she stooped to pick up a piece, she heard the zing of a bullet ricochet off the side of the rock above her head.

"Get down!"

She whirled, and Roark stepped from behind a ledge. He threw himself down taking Jade with him as another bullet cracked through the silence, and then he was firing his revolver. The shattering noise made Jade wince.

She spat gravel from her mouth as she cringed

78

against the dirt, feeling the weight of Roark's arm around her holding her tightly.

For a few minutes they didn't move, and the guns were silent. Jade buried her face against his arm until it passed. The wind rushed down the mountain and stirred up the dust.

"Who's firing at us?" she gasped.

"Somebody who doesn't want us here," he replied dryly. "I'd like to know what you're doing? I asked Samuel to keep you away."

Jade recoiled at the authoritative scold in his voice. "I don't take orders from you, sir. It's my father's claim. I have a right to be here."

"Tell that to the man who's shooting at us. I don't think he'll be impressed with your independence—or your claim."

"All right. So I should have been more careful. Thanks for getting me out of the way. But that's no reason to keep me pinned down here. Maybe he's gone."

Jade strained to listen and heard nothing but the wind stirring among the rocks and rustling the sage.

"We can't take a chance with a rifle. We'll need to wait an hour or so at least."

"You expect me to lay like this for an hour?"

"Sorry. Serves you right for coming out here."

"You sound very sympathetic. Am I finally meeting the real Roark Montgomery?"

"You met him a long time ago. I didn't know there was more than one."

"I didn't either, until I discovered from Samuel how you tricked me to get information about my father!"

79

"The information you gave me about Thomas made no difference."

"Then you admit you used me to find him!"

"I haven't found him yet. Evidently, the person shooting that rifle hasn't either."

She raised her face to retort, but suddenly realized there were only inches between them. The words choked into silence as she found herself staring into warm blue-gray eyes narrowing under dark lashes. Her face flushed. "Let go of me."

"A man has a rifle pinned on us. I wouldn't exactly call this 'holding hands in the moonlight'." He glanced back up at the ridge.

Jade turned her head away, angry with herself for overreacting. Now she had revealed her feelings. If his nearness hadn't distracted her so, she wouldn't have responded so abruptly.

For an hour, Roark waited, but no additional shots were fired. The late afternoon sun was dipping down behind the far hills when finally he said, "He's gone," and took his arm away. Jade sat up, brushing off her dress. Avoiding his eyes, she jumped to her feet, walked to her mule, and unloosed her art satchel with deliberate movements.

"Now, what do you think you're going to do?"

Jade didn't answer. She proceeded to set up a flimsy easel, gathered a pad and pencil, and settled back on a smooth rock.

His mouth curved, and he pushed his hat back. "My dear girl, is it not enough that you nearly got blasted with a rifle? Are you going to sit there like a target?"

She refused to look at him and began to sketch the mountain ridge above the stone hut as if she had not a care in the world. "I don't know why anyone would want to be shooting at me. I'm sure he saw you and decided a no-account lawman from San Francisco would be better stewed as a jackrabbit."

"I'll ignore that, madam." He walked up. "As for no one wishing to shoot at you, you're wrong. You're the daughter of Thomas O'Neil, and he's not very popular around here at the moment."

Jade didn't flinch. She had accepted the ugly situation to be as inevitable as her illness.

"The Ramos brothers think he's Jack Dawson. I'm looked upon as Samuel's niece."

"I wish it were that easy. They've learned who your father is. That makes you unwanted company. If the claim holds up, and something happens to Thomas, you're the heir."

Heir to a silver mine! Jade's eyes widened at the thought, and she forced her mind away from even considering the possibility. She showed no excitement and continued to sketch. Roark didn't know it, but she was sketching him, and she was venting her internal frustration.

"But don't get your hopes up. According to Bill Stewert, the claim probably belongs to the brothers."

"I'm sure you'd be the first to say my father stole it from them."

"I'd like to be the last. Do you think I'm enjoying this?"

"Yes, I do. You hate my father, and—"

"You're wrong."

Suddenly the wind swept down and overturned the easel, sending her things flying. She let out a cry and tried to grab them, but they went in all directions. As Roark helped, they salvaged most of it, and Roark looked at the sketch she had been doing of him. His eyes met hers, and his brows shot up.

"If this is the best you can do, you'll never sell anything."

The wind was growing bitter cold and she drew her cloak about her. As she stared defiantly into his eyes, he looked anything but the villain of her sketch. He was too handsome, she told herself quickly.

"This is a miserable time to sketch," he added. "What's the real reason you rode out here?"

Jade turned and walked in the direction of the stone hut. "I've come to lay claim to my father's cabin. You'll have to move out."

"You can't move in here. It's too dangerous."

"We can't stay the winter with Samuel. Holly's already complaining about privacy."

"You remember those rifle shots? Do you want Shaun running around out here? I know you better than that, Jade. Why did you come?"

"To sketch. I plan on making a living the only way I can."

"Commendable ambition. I think I told you before that you should make use of the talent the Lord gave you. But you didn't come here today to sketch."

She turned swiftly. "Well, I certainly didn't come here to see you."

He reached over and swung open the cabin door. His slight smile was better left ignored, she told herself, and walked inside past him, looking about. It wasn't much. A cot, a table, and a small open fireplace to cook on. She turned back to him. "I'm also curious about the mine and what the Ramos brothers are looking for. I don't suppose you'd tell me?"

"There is no mine, not yet, just some diggings. However, I took a look at them and they appear to be rich in ore."

"Do you think my father jumped their claim?"

He didn't flinch. "There's reason to believe he did. And he's got three gunslingers from Utah to back him up."

"You're so sure my father is guilty!"

"Yes, Jade, I am. I'm sorry."

She almost believed he was and turned away. For some reason she felt less vulnerable when she believed Roark an unfeeling tyrant.

"You know what they're looking for, don't you?"

For a moment he said nothing, just silently watched her. "You want me to be honest with you, Jade, and I will, even though you'll find it painful." He took out the torn sheet of paper Samuel had given him. "This is the only evidence of who may own this claim. The fact that it's written in pencil, and has names and dates erased and rewritten, means a long court battle."

The paper didn't appear important to Jade. Certainly nothing to be shooting over. "You think my father erased the name of the Ramos brothers, and wrote his own in?"

"It's possible, but whatever the law decides about this claim, he's still a wanted man in San Francisco. The only difference is, if the claim proves rightfully his, you'll be the heir. So I've taken it to Bill Stewert, the lawyer."

"I don't want the claim, not if men must die over it."

"I know you well enough to understand that," he said softly. "Your father and the Ramos brothers won't prove as wise. That means someone's going to get hurt. Now do you see why I don't want you here?"

"But it's all right if they shoot at you, is that it?"

"Don't tell me you're concerned?" he asked with mock delight.

"When you're determined to arrest my father? No."

He leaned his shoulder against the open door and watched her from under his hat. "I'll get my horse and ride back with you."

"You needn't bother. I know the way."

"It's getting dark, and I want to talk with Samuel. I might as well leave for a few days and let them take a good look in the cabin. They won't find anything. The one hint of legality is in this paper. And they don't know I've got it."

They said nothing on the ride back until they neared Sun Mountain. As Jade dismounted from the mule, she asked, "What do you want to see Samuel about?"

"Building a cabin."

"I thought you were staying on at Seven-Mile?"

"The cabin's for you."

Her mouth opened then shut. Surely he was jesting. Roark, build her a cabin?

He looked around. "Over there's a fair spot if it's not claimed."

"I don't want you to build me a cabin. I haven't paid you the money I owe you yet, Mr. Montgomery."

"Let's not bicker over trifles, Miss O'Neil. Winter's coming. If you insist on staying in Virginia City against my advice, you'll need a warm place to stay. And, I want you close by Samuel."

Jade floundered for a moment, trying to understand his actions and her feelings, but gazing up into his eyes revealed nothing but a relaxed, even stare.

By the next day, Roark had acquired the land and the building process was under way. To her utter amazement, a three room structure was put together in days. During that time she watched him working with Samuel, working hard and not seeming to mind at all.

Holly went out of her way to pay tribute for, unlike Jade, she had no quarrel with him over his duty to arrest Thomas. "If Pa is innocent," she had said, "the jury will acquit him." And Shaun, who knew nothing of the lurid details, was drawn to Roark more than ever. Only Jade was quiet as he and Samuel carried in the last of their meager belongings two weeks later.

"Now, if we just had something to sit on," Holly said wistfully.

"Barrels will make fine chairs," said Samuel, "if we can get Toby here to fix a few." He turned to the old miner. "You're good with your hands, and this is better than mucking. Maybe you can come up with a table, as well."

"For some of Miss Holly's biscuits and stew, I'll make her a whole room o' furniture."

Holly smiled and seemed genuinely pleased with her new ability to cook. "This spring when Dave—I mean Mr. Wylet—runs the mule train over the Sierras again, he's going to loan me the money to start an eatery. It doesn't look as if Aunt Norma's going to write us from New York."

"That's a great idea, Holly," said Samuel.

"I'll help make the gingerbread cakes," said Shaun.

"You'll be too busy," said Jade with a smile. "I'm going to start your arithmetic lessons again."

"Oh, Jade!"

Samuel gestured out the front door. "Well, Roark, looks like the Lord let us just make it!"

They all turned to look and saw rain pelting the soil. Jade sat on a barrel, trying to mask the weariness that ravaged her body. Her eyes watched the raindrops become a heavy torrent and turn the alkali into oozing mud. Feeling cold, she drew her shawl about her.

"There's snow in the wind," Roark was telling Samuel. "We'll need to get a good supply of wood and food. There'll be a scramble for the stock on hand once the snow hits. The mule trains won't be able to make it in."

"I'll ride with you to Carson."

"Carson?" asked Holly, suddenly alert. "Then would you tell Mr. Wylet he's invited to Sunday dinner?"

"After Uncle Samuel gets done preaching for two hours, we'll all be starved," said Shaun.

They laughed and Samuel grabbed the feather-weight boy, swinging him up onto his shoulders. "Just for that, lad, you're coming to Carson with us."

Holly followed Samuel out the door, telling him everything she needed for the kitchen.

My! But Holly's changed! thought Jade, pleased. Dave Wylet had apparently captured her heart and set it to music.

"Anything I can get you?"

She turned at Roark's voice; she'd forgotten he was standing there. There was something, but Jade hesitated to mention it. The craving she felt was rather embarrassing. Besides, she owed him too much money already.

"Well. . . ," she paused and touched her curls. "If you see any—chocolate—you might buy some."

"Chocolate," he repeated. "For Shaun, of course. . . . Shall I add that to your account?"

Jade got up from the barrel and walked into the

bedroom. She heard him laugh to himself as the door shut behind him. It was quiet except for the rain beating on the roof. She looked up, half expecting it to start leaking, but it was dry, private, and compared to the outdoors, warm. If it hadn't been for Roark, she would still be cramped together with Holly and Shaun in Uncle Samuel's dugout.

A few minutes later she heard Holly come into the room.

"Now that we're alone, Jade O'Neil, I'm going to tell you what I think of you."

"What on earth—" Jade turned to her sister, surprised by the firmness of her voice. Holly's blue eyes were fixed on her, and her hands were on her hips.

"Whatever is the matter with you—"

Holly interrupted. "I'll tell you what's the matter. You're behaving like a spoiled brat."

Jade sucked in her breath. "Me! Spoiled?"

"Yes, you," said Holly. "Being a woman I'll tell you what Uncle Samuel won't. Roark Montgomery's falling in love with you, and you're crazy if you let a man like that slip through your fingers."

Jade stared at her sister for a long moment in stunned silence. "In love with me?" Jade laughed shortly. "Are you mad? He's here to arrest Pa. It's the only reason he's staying on. That, and because it's too late in the season to travel the Sierras."

"I suspect if Roark wanted to get across the Sierras in the dead of winter, he could manage. I say he's staying because he's worried about you."

"His reasons for staying in Virginia City have nothing to do with me."

"Roark's bending backward to be nice to you, and

you're treating him miserably!" Holly accused.

"He intends to arrest father."

"Maybe it's best he does."

"Holly!'

"Well, suppose Pa hurts someone else?"

"We don't know if he's hurt anyone."

"As for Roark—who else would work and sweat to build this private room for you? Do you see any other men willing to get tired for you?"

"Holly—"

"No, you need to hear this, Jade; you need to do some serious thinking before it's too late. Who else would concern himself with your warmth, and your supper table, and your health?"

Jade stared at her, unable to reply.

"And you don't even speak politely to him. It's you who's not showing Christian virtue, yet you feel justified to act this way toward him because he's bound by an oath to uphold the law that Pa disobeyed."

Jade was miserable. "I—I just don't want to get hurt again, Holly. Not after St. Louis, not after Beau."

"Go ahead then," Holly said quietly. "Build a wall around yourself. But you'll learn that it will hurt just as much behind your garrison."

Chapter 7

Holly's words hurt, but Jade refused to dwell on them. For the next two weeks she gave herself entirely to capturing on canvas as much of the life of the mining community as the weather would allow. The town was small enough to cover on foot and, climbing from A to D street, she was seen mornings and afternoons carrying her satchel to some spot where she could be alone to sketch the mood of Virginia City.

It never occurred to her when Roark Montgomery just "happened" to ride by during her daily excursions that it was anything more than an accident. At first she treated him with coolness, but his attentiveness became more and more difficult to resist.

"Why aren't you out at Seven-Mile? Aren't you afraid you'll miss my father?" she asked coolly one day.

He calmly reached under his jacket and removed his badge.

Jade's eyes widened. "Roark! What are you doing?"

"I'm going to toss it over the hill. Forget Thomas O'Neil. Forget everything. I'm going to ride out of Virginia City without a second look behind, and I'm going to take you with me to see Dr. Montgomery."

Stunned, she stared up at him. "You'd do that for me?"

"I might. . .if you'd ask me. You'd lay aside your bitterness if I did, wouldn't you?"

For a confused moment she couldn't speak. She watched the wind tug at his jacket, seeing again clearly that he embodied everything in a man she wanted. The realization brought a choked feeling to her throat, and her dark lashes flickered above her delicate cheeks. At last she found her voice.

"You can't simply throw away what you are by getting rid of your badge!"

"No? Why not?"

She searched his face; it was unreadable. Was he serious?

"Because," she said quietly, "you took an oath to uphold the law."

"That oath includes upholding the law no matter who's involved," he reminded her, "even if it's your father."

Jade didn't want to hear anymore. She knew he was right, but she feared that her true feelings for him would be displayed.

"I'd rather not discuss my father. You will do what you must, what your conscience before God tells you. And I," she said, "will also do what I came here for."

"And if we each do what we feel we must, does that

mean we can't be civil to each other, or share a little company? After all, Miss O'Neil, I do have somewhat of an investment in you."

She felt her face turn warm and turned away. She didn't see his subdued amusement. "You aren't at all gallant to bring up my indebtedness. I assure you, I intend to pay back every penny as soon as *The Enterprise* buys some of my sketches."

"The town newspaper isn't likely to be buying sketches," he said smoothly. "But the San Francisco newspaper might. It so happens the editor is a friend of mine. That's what I want to talk to you about. As yet, I haven't seen much of your work. If it's good, I might be able to interest him. Suppose you show me what you've done over dinner tonight?"

Her heart raced. The San Francisco newspaper! For a moment her grandest dream was coming true! Then her brows came together. "Why is it that every time I need something, you have the key?"

His smile was disarming. "Why don't you ask the Lord about that?"

Her green eyes scanned him then, turning, she started uphill toward Maguire's Opera House. The climb was not difficult, but on a cold day her lungs burned from physical exertion. She was soon out of breath and miserable. The simple uphill walk left her dizzy.

Roark prompted his horse ahead and came up beside her. He took his foot from the stirrup and smiled. "Ride?"

He was hard to resist, and at times she thought he knew it. She smiled ruefully and thrust her satchel at him, then stepped up without a word.

91

"Where to, my lady? The Court of St. James?" he jested.

"Maguire's Opera House will do nicely, kind sir. Roark? Is it to escort me that you show up like this?" she asked decidedly.

He laughed, and his eyes danced with amusement. "What! You mean you've guessed! How wise of you, and how clumsy of me. I thought surely no one would ever suspect my secret intentions! You know, you really shouldn't be wandering around alone."

"I suppose San Francisco has no fast guns, gambling, or opium dens like Virginia City?"

He frowned. "Who told you about the opium dens?"

"Samuel. I suppose you still think I'm too young to know of such things?"

"Knowing you, you'd think nothing of going there to get a good sketch."

"Samuel is concerned about the despicable things going on."

"As well he should be."

"If I could, I'd like to help those Oriental women who are sold like slaves—" She stopped and looked at him directly. "I don't suppose you'd pin your badge plainly on the front of your jacket, and escort me—"

"Absolutely not. I'm sure Samuel never suggested you carry your Bible in there and try to open up a Sunday School."

"Somebody has to bring them the gospel. If we don't, who will? I don't see anyone else concerned for their souls."

"Your concern is well taken. But I'll be blunt. You could get into deep trouble. They're not above a white-slave market. You could disappear there, and no one would ever find you again."

Jade lapsed into silence.

"If they listen at all, it will be to Samuel. I hear that Hop Sing has invited him to meet privately with the top merchants."

Jade tried to appear undaunted. "Well, if you won't take me, then I suppose I'll need to be satisfied with the Piutes."

He laughed so loudly that she wondered what he found so amusing.

"Do they really have dried scalps hanging from their girdles?"

"They do. Do you plan on sketching a few of them as well?"

"I'll settle for Chief Winnemucca sitting astride his horse. Samuel expects to pay him a pow-wow one of these days, and I intend to go with him."

"Not if I have anything to do with it. The Forty-Mile is no place for you."

"You'll never see me as anything but a school girl, will you?"

"I'll talk to Samuel and warn him not to let you go."

"If you do, Roark Montgomery, I'll never speak to you again."

"Look over there at the Sierras, majestic and crowned with white. Why don't you feast your appetite on that?"

"I've already painted the Sierras. Now I want to capture the personality of the people who have come to Washoe: Miners, fast guns, Samuel, the Piutes, the girl with the rifle—"

" 'Girl with the rifle'?"

"A young woman I saw at Strawberry. I admired her

spirit. She was strong, the way I want to be."

"Ah. . .the girl who won the wrestling match. So you wish to—"

"And a certain lawman with pistols peeping from his belt," she continued smoothly.

"You mean you've graciously decided to re-do the villain you sketched at Seven-Mile? Well! I knew you'd eventually come to see just what a gallant man Roark Montgomery is!"

She turned and looked up at him, intending to be as light and indifferent as he was, but as their eyes met, she fell into confusion. The warmth of his gaze held hers. What would it be like to have him dip her backward over his arm just so and then—

"Did Beau ever tell you that your eyes are like soft emeralds?"

"No," she murmured. "He talked about—Indians."

"How very imaginative of him. You mean a young girl never got bored after so many walks in the St. Louis moonlight discussing anthropology?"

"We never walked in the moonlight. . . .I think—" and she paused when his eyes drifted to her lips.

"I think, my dear," he said silkily, "that this is the perfect spot to sketch the Opera House."

He dismounted and helped her down. He glanced up at the sky as he carried her satchel. "You'll need to work fast. Looks like snow."

"Oh it does, doesn't it? Here, help me set up my easel. I hope the wind doesn't blow my things over again."

Dusk was falling over Virginia City when she finished, and they walked down C Street. With its myriad of lamps and campfires, it seemed to be tiered with a string of Christmas candles.

94

"Look, Roark, doesn't the mountain remind you of a giant Christmas tree?"

"I've seen better," he said wryly.

The saloons were crowded, and piano music drifted from the doors, but the atmosphere in the International Hotel was pleasant. The large table was covered with a fine cloth and spread with so many dishes that it reminded Jade of past Christmas dinners in St. Louis. She ate everything on her plate for the first time in months.

Afterward, Roark took his time leafing through her sketches. For over ten minutes he did not say a word.

"Well?" she asked when she couldn't stand it any longer. "Do you like them or not?"

"Excellent."

"You mean that?"

He looked up. "Of course, I mean it. I don't flatter to make you feel good. I like your style—and your message."

"Then you could tell I was trying to say something in my work, that I wasn't just drawing attractive scenes."

"I saw it at once. . .have you taken lessons?"

"Well—no."

"I saw that, too. But you do have talent, a great deal of it."

"Then you'll show them to the San Francisco editor?"

He smiled. "Only if you come with me to see my father."

"It really isn't fair to bribe me. You know that, don't you?'

"If the editor's unable to use them, he'll know of a

95

magazine in the East that will. They're hungry to know everything about the West. It affords them amusement.

"Unfortunately, going there is out of the question until spring. Looks as if I'll be staying the winter in town." He sobered. "And that brings me to the other matter we need to discuss."

Jade guessed what was coming. The evening had been enjoyable, and Roark had proved to be exciting company. For a few hours, she had forgotten her father. Now it all came rushing back.

"I'd rather not discuss my father, Roark."

His voice was quiet but resolved. "We must. We've been letting this slide too long. Your father will return for the paper he left with Samuel. When he does, I'll have to arrest him."

"My father may not even show up for the paper."

"Even without it, he'll try to take control of the claim. When he does, the Ramos brothers will be around to stop him."

"And you must stop them all, is that it?"

"It's my job."

He couldn't be as cool as he appeared, she thought, or was he? His suave manner gave her no reason to suspect otherwise. In frustration she blurted out the obvious.

"Your job may get you killed!"

A trace of humor showed on his mouth.

Knowing she had betrayed herself again, she challenged, "And so you expect to take on the Ramos brothers *and* the three men from Salt Lake?"

"I expect to find your father before they do. It's his best chance of coming out of this alive, and before that happens, I want you out of Virginia City."

"I'm not leaving."

For a moment stormy green eyes locked with determined blue-gray ones.

"Until I know my father's guilty of killing a man, I'll wait before I rush to be his judge and jury."

"He'll get a fair trial in San Francisco. I'll see to that."

"Will you? You're sure of your own feelings, Roark?"

She saw a flicker of temper. It was one of the few times she had seen a flaw in his armor.

"These past weeks have been frustrating, but are you insinuating that I'd enjoy going to his hanging?"

Her own frustration poured out, too. "What do you think it's been like for me? It's my father you're tracking like some wounded wolf bleeding in the snow."

"Picturesque, my dear, but not entirely accurate. He nearly blew my head off with a rifle."

"You think it was my father out at Seven-Mile? Shooting at *me*? I don't believe it!"

"The incident I'm referring to happened again yesterday."

"Did you see him?"

"No."

"Then you've no proof. You *want* it to be my father."

"So now I'm on a selfish crusade of cold-blooded vengeance."

Frustrated, she breathed, "I didn't say that."

"Am I to throw justice aside because the man's your father? Has Thomas cared enough for any of you in the past six years to keep in touch, or to take care of his wife?"

Their words seemed to tighten around them as they

stared unrelentingly at each other. Jade was squeezing the napkin in her lap into a damp knot. Unable to control herself any longer, she threw it down on the table and stood to leave. Roark stood, too, and caught her wrist.

"Wait. . .I lost my temper. I'm sorry."

"Words that speak truth shouldn't be hurled like daggers. Or does that bit of sin not mean anything? It's only my father's unscrupulous ways that are evil!"

"Now you're throwing daggers."

Aware that heads had turned in their direction, Jade sat down.

"As to your remark, yes," she stated. "We've all wondered a thousand times where he was when we needed him, when mother needed him. If we thought too long, it brought confusion and pain. It was that way in St. Louis; it's true here in Virginia City. Shaun constantly badgers me with questions about where his Pa is, and why we can't go visit him at 'his mine' and help him dig for silver. He thinks his father is everything that you are. How do you expect me to tell him that he's not? And that it's you who arrested him?"

He reached across the table and took her hand. Jade started to pull away, but found his touch radiated an understanding she wanted. *I won't cry like a baby,* she told herself. *He already thinks I'm one.*

"I'll talk to Shaun when the time comes. Samuel, too, will know what to say. I've already seen a deep bond forming between the boy and his uncle. But, Jade, I can't compromise what's right because of personal feelings. I took an oath before I came. I'm under the governor's authority."

She searched his face and saw that his gaze was calm again, and she could not deny his statement. If he was telling the truth now, then why not about everything else, including her father's guilt?

"I don't hate your father, Jade."

"When you're convinced he shot your father?"

"I admit I did hate him at first. That was three years ago. My father was wounded because of some cheap card game he wasn't even playing in. Even though I knew better, I did hate the gambler named Thomas O'Neil. I hated enough to strike back as hard as he had struck my father."

"Please, I don't want to hear the details—"

"I want you to hear them, Jade. My father was a fine physician, a skilled surgeon. His steady hand under God's control had saved many lives. And when I saw his wrist shot to pieces—" He stopped to control his emotion.

Jade lowered her head and shut her eyes. The thought that her father could be to blame for something so awful made her feel sick.

Roark controlled himself. "It was then that I left medical school. I *was* bitter. Even though I knew Christ as my Saviour, carried a Bible, and prayed, I had a hot temper. It never dawned on me that my quest for justice was nothing more than revenge. I hunted him through Texas and into St. Louis; I may even have seen you one Sunday at a church I dropped into."

She looked up, startled.

"You wore a green satin dress. . .you were with a blond man, young, quiet—"

"Beau Wilson."

"I can't remember what the minister talked about that morning, but when I came back to San Francisco, the anger driving me was slowly diminishing, like some refreshing breeze from heaven had moved within. I

99

realized that the Lord had a purpose behind what happened to my father. It was time to trust."

Jade couldn't speak. She was ashamed, yet thankful that neither Roark nor his father had been swallowed up by the bitterness of their trials. She felt a stirring within. *Please, Father, don't let me be destroyed either.*

"It isn't easy to overcome bitterness," she said.

"I finally came to understand and accept that there are reasons for our disappointments. My father's ability as a physician has changed from surgery—to the study of tuberculosis. He's doing research, and he has some exciting plans to open a sanitarium for patients in the West someplace where the winters are dry and clear. I would say the Lord's hand is evident in all our circumstances."

"I don't think your father would be interested in treating the daughter of the man who destroyed his hand."

"Never underestimate the grace of God. My father is not bitter. He's a man of faith. I'd like for you to meet him."

Jade sat silently, her emotions pulling in two directions at once. After several minutes, she saw Roark's jaw tighten. He stood and tossed some money down on the table. He looked out the window.

"Looks like the storm's finally blowing in. I'll see you back to the cabin."

Chapter 8

As Roark and Jade walked out of the hotel, Bill Ramos stepped from the shadows near the Delta gambling hall. His deep-set eyes were riveted on Roark, and his hand flexed as he lowered it toward his holster.

Across the street a second man, Ramon Ramos, stepped down from the boardwalk.

"Montgomery!" Bill Ramos's voice split the night.

Roark instinctively knew the feel of danger. He pushed Jade back toward the shadowed building. "Get down."

"Where's the paper Thomas gave the old preacher?" Ramos called. "I want it!"

The street began to clear.

"Leave the claim to arbitration. You'll live longer," warned Roark.

Bill Ramos walked toward him, and Roark heard slow steps coming from the other direction. His hand moved into position.

"Don't be a fool, Ramos. You're not ready to die."

"Don't start that! I don't want to hear it! I want the paper!"

Just then, Roark's eyes caught several men on the roofs of two buildings across the street. By the way they raised their rifles, he knew they were not with the two brothers.

"Watch out, Ramos! Behind you!"

Ramos didn't believe him. Instead, he drew and fired, but Roark beat him by a hair, striking his gunhand. Then, the rifles flashed from the rooftop across the street and struck Ramos in the back. Roark dove for the ground as a blast of bullets sprayed in all directions. When it was over, Ramon Ramos lay dead with his brother, and one man had fallen from the roof. The faint, acrid odor of powder smoke hung in the air. The quiet was shattering.

The empty piano music started up again, and the moment went as unheeded as a yawn.

Roark raced toward Jade. "You all right, Jade?"

Her numbed eyes focused on his face, but she didn't answer. He lifted her up, and she clung to him. He held her close for another moment.

"You're not hurt?" she whispered, her voice shaking.

"No. I'm fine. Wait here, though. I want to see who fell from the roof."

Roark crossed the narrow street and bent over the man. In the dim light he saw that it was Letterman, the gunslinger he had talked to at Berry's Flat. Roark knew Jesse and his brother Ernie must have been the other two on the roof, sent by Thomas to eliminate the

Ramos brothers and solidify his claim to the diggings at Seven-Mile. So far, two of the brothers were dead. . . that left Kidd.

Jade was waiting when Roark returned to her side. "Did you know that man?"

"Letterman."

"Were they after you, Roark?"

"Not this time." He took her arm. "Come, I'll take you home."

"Suppose those men are waiting out there in the dark?"

"My guess is they'll not be so easy to find, not after tonight. They'll lay up for awhile until things calm down."

"If they killed the Ramos brothers to get them out of the way, that only leaves the younger brother—and you."

"Looks that way, doesn't it."

"How can you be so calm?" she gritted.

"Because I intend to be careful. I'm going to find Thomas before the two men working for him find me."

A bitter wind was sweeping down from Sun Mountain, sending violent gusts of bitter air against them.

"You shouldn't be out in this," he said. "When we get to the cabin, I suggest you go to bed. I'll tell Samuel what happened tonight."

As they approached the cabin, the glow in the windows showed that Holly and Shaun were up. Jade tried to control her shaking.

"You think my father had something to do with this, don't you?" she asked, as they stopped at the door of the cabin.

103

"My guess is that the men on the roof were following his orders. They've probably been promised a few feet in the claim for their guns."

Was he too quick to conclude that her father was involved? She felt the blast of cold wind sting her face. Inside she felt cold, too.

He turned to walk away.

"Roark! Where are you going now?"

"To see Samuel."

"I'm coming with you."

"Stay here, Jade."

"If my father's what you say he is—if he was behind those deaths tonight and wants to kill you, too—then I'm going to find him. I'll make him give himself up."

"If he won't listen to Samuel, he won't listen to you. And I won't have you getting hurt. I mean it, Jade, if you try anything foolish—"

"Foolish! Is that what you think of me?"

"No, that's *not* what I think of you."

She stopped short. For a moment he stared down at her so intensely that she couldn't speak. Then, abruptly, he turned and walked to his horse.

She watched him untie the reins and walk away, toward Samuel's dugout.

When Jade entered the cabin, the wind caught the door from her hand and blew it shut. Holly stood quickly. "Jade, what on earth! Here, sit by the fire. You're so pale. And you're shaking!"

She sank against the door "Where's Shaun?"

"In bed. What's happened, Jade?"

Jade described the gunfight. Holly was almost speechless, her eyes questioning the outcome. "I've got a feeling this ordeal with Pa isn't going to end easily."

"I've got to find Pa before something worse happens."

"Find Pa? But how? We've been here since October, and he hasn't shown himself. If Roark and Samuel don't know where he is, how do you expect to find him?"

"I don't know, but I'm going to try."

The days passed, but Holly's statement proved to be true. If Thomas O'Neil was somewhere in the vicinity of Virginia City, he kept his presence a secret. And Jade's own search for her father had proved entirely futile.

Exhausted from her latest tour of the gambling halls inquiring for anyone who knew "Jack Dawson," she was returning to Samuel's dugout when she saw Roark's horse tied nearby. She didn't mean to eavesdrop, but Samuel's voice boomed out from the entrance, and she caught the word "Winnemucca. . . ."

". . .This is something I've worked and prayed long and hard for, lad. The Lord's opened a door to teach."

"When are you leaving?"

"In the morning."

"Jade will want to go. In her condition, I don't think it would be wise. Besides, it may prove dangerous. . . ."

Jade's heart began to pound. A meeting with the Chief of the Piutes! What a sketch Samuel and Winnemucca would make! *I've got to have it!* she thought, as she walked inside the dugout. A pot of coffee and a plate of Holly's ginger cakes was on the table. She poured herself a cup, picked up a cake, and sat down. Roark was leaning against the wall. She couldn't wait to let him know that he had underestimated her.

"Well, lass, where have you been all morning?" Samuel asked.

"Looking for my father. I've covered every gambling hall in town—again."

From the corner of her eye she saw Roark look quickly in her direction, but she pretended not to notice.

"Samuel," said Roark smoothly, "didn't you teach your niece that gambling halls are no place for a young lady?"

Samuel scowled over at her. "He's right, lass. What were you doing in the taverns alone?"

"You needn't look so alarmed, Uncle Samuel. Most of the men, like Mr. Montgomery, think of me only as a child." And then she dropped the dynamite smoothly. "But I did learn where my father was."

"What!" cried Samuel, jumping to his feet. "You know were Tommy is?"

Roark straightened up and looked down at her. She saw the uncertainty in his eyes. He didn't know whether to believe her or not.

"A man by the name of Spafford Hall has spoken with him recently."

Samuel turned to Roark. "Spafford Hall's Station is near the Carson River."

"I know the place. Who told you this, Jade?"

She drew in a breath, wondering what his reaction would be. She was treading new territory where his emotions were concerned. "Kidd Ramos."

His eyes turned slate colored, the way they did when he was angry, and his jaw set. "You talked to Ramos!

He's a hothead with a gun! And he has a reputation with women to match. Did you tell him you were O'Neil's daughter?"

"No, and I did learn some useful information. That's more than you gave me credit for—"

"Samuel," he interrupted, "if you don't keep her out of this, she's going to get hurt. Ramos is not a man to play with!"

"Yes, yes, lad," Samuel said. "I'll see that it doesn't happen again."

Jade was not only disappointed, but she felt an uncomfortable twinge of guilt. Her actions had angered him more than she had anticipated. She decided quickly that there was no feeling of satisfaction in provoking him.

She stood to her feet. "I didn't mean to get you and Samuel so angry. I was only trying to—"

"I know what you were trying to do," he interrupted coldly. "I don't need your detective work, Jade."

She felt herself flush, but he didn't appear to notice. "If Kidd Ramos had known who you were, he might have held you for ransom, the payoff being the delivery of Thomas. Do you realize the dilemma that would have put me in? Not to mention your danger?"

She hadn't, of course, and now that he mentioned it—taking no caution with the way he addressed her— Jade felt irritated with herself. His words stung and, afraid she would show how much, she brushed past him and out the entrance of the dugout.

Jade O'Neil, you're an idiot, she told herself, and hurried in the direction of the cabin. She threw open the door and stormed in; Holly and Shaun were gone. In trying to prove herself capable, she had only managed to do the opposite. She threw her cloak down upon the table. It crossed her mind that the one time Roark had appeared impressed was when she had begun a women's Bible class several weeks before, and the "girl with the rifle" had attended.

She turned at a quick knock at the door in time to see it open. Roark stood there staring at her. She just looked at him, and for a long moment, the silence grew. Then he sighed and pushed his hat back a little.

"I'm sorry I lost my temper. I was rude."

The fact that he had come brought sweet satisfaction. For a moment the words wouldn't come. Then she smiled ruefully. "When you said last night that you had a temper, you weren't exaggerating, were you?" she asked quietly.

His brows slanted. "No, I wasn't. But it takes something I really care about to get me upset. Not that it's an excuse."

She was beginning to enjoy herself. She folded her arms and sat down on the edge of the table. Her green eyes surveyed him. "So, Roark Montgomery has weak spots in his armor, after all. He has a temper, and he can be domineering."

He leaned his shoulder in the doorway and watched her. "I confess."

She smiled, her eyes teasing his. "I forgive you for your vices."

"Thank you." His eyes challenged her. "I forgive yours as well."

"Thank you."

"And I admit your detective work was well done, Miss O'Neil, even if it was unwise." Before she could reply, he smiled, turned, and walked away as unexpectedly as he had come.

The next morning was Sunday, but Jade was too restless to concentrate on Samuel's message. Winnemucca! She must have the sketch! Oh, the San Francisco newspaper would love it! When the service had ended, she escaped Holly and Shaun, leaving them with Dave Wylet, and hurried into the cabin. In a few minutes she had changed into her riding clothes and, with a satchel in hand, went to where the mule was waiting.

When Samuel arrived and saw her mounted, his eyes narrowed. Knowing he guessed her intentions she sighed.

"Please, Uncle Samuel. I'm going with you to meet Chief Winnemucca. This is the painting of a lifetime, and I simply *must* have it."

He scowled and shook his dark head. "Too dangerous, lass."

Jade pressed. "I'll keep a safe distance from your pow-wow. All I need is about twenty minutes to sketch the scene. Roark promised to show my work to an editor he knows in San Francisco."

"After yesterday he might change his mind," he suggested with a teasing glint to his eye.

"A sketch of Preacher Samuel with Winnemucca is worth any risk or ride to the Forty-Mile."

"Hah."

"It's a chance I'm willing to take."

"But not your ol' uncle. I won't hear of it, Jade. There's talk of trouble with the Piutes."

"Samuel! I've got to get that sketch!"

He scowled again, his eyes quizzing hers.

"Lass, you don't know what you're asking me."

"Uncle Samuel, you can't turn me down. I came to Virginia City with the Indians in mind. I knew well the danger it could pose. You know I may not live to be a grandmother, not with this illness. So let me spend my remaining years doing what I feel strongly about."

"What's this? Talking like a woman with a last request already? A young girl hardly out of her teens?"

"Samuel," she said wearily, "you're just like Roark. I've been out of my teens for years. I'm almost twenty-three, yet he insists on treating me like Shaun."

"A mere fledgling," said Samuel.

"One who wishes to spread her wings."

"Over Piute territory."

"Samuel, I've set my heart on going. You wouldn't turn me down now, would you?"

"It's bad territory, Jade. The dust wouldn't be good for you."

"I've brought a bandana. Please, Uncle Samuel!"

He scowled. "Montgomery's not going to like this."

"Roark? You mean he's going?"

"He's meeting me at the Carson River."

Jade squirmed a little in the saddle. "Well, he'll just have to accept the idea that I'm going to get my sketch."

"How is it, lass, that you get your way with me?"

She smiled down into his bearded face. "Maybe we've got more in common than you realize."

"All right, lass, but don't say I didn't warn you."

Chapter 9

The alkali dust of Twelve-Mile Canyon toward
Spafford Hall's Station on the Carson River was stifling.
Despite the scarf around her nose and mouth, Jade
could taste the bitter saltiness. The constant wind
kicked up a cloud of white dust.

Samuel was riding a short distance ahead of her
when he paused and called back. "Montgomery's
ahead, lass. Wait here until I explain. He's going to be
blistering mad at me for bringing you."

Nodding, Jade stopped her mule and waited.
Adjusting her scarf, she watched Roark ride up to meet
Samuel. She could see them talking, but the wind
carried their voices away from her.

A minute later Roark rode up to her. His dark jacket
was dusted with the whitish alkali, and his hat was
pulled low. He wore a slight smile, and flicked the reins

111

across his gloved hand.

"Why, Miss O'Neil, what a pleasant surprise."

"Yes, isn't it," she said sweetly, and smiled. "I'm going to get the best sketch the San Francisco newspaper will see in years."

"The worst part of our journey, is ahead. The Humboldt River and the Forty-Mile Desert. Men have died crossing it from Utah. The wind gusts can take you off your mule, and the wasteland is littered with bleached bones and old wagons. I'm not risking you to a meeting with the Piutes."

"I understand what you must have gone through with your grandparents, but this is different. Roark, I need that sketch desperately! I'll never get another opportunity like this."

He was silent for a moment. "It really means that much to you, doesn't it?"

"You know it does."

He smiled. "Yes, I do know. . . .All right. I'll see that you get your sketch of Winnemucca."

"I knew I could depend on you."

"Did you?"

"Yes. . .I'm beginning to understand you."

"That could be dangerous."

"To me?"

"No, to me."

Roark looked in the direction of Spafford's Station. Jade turned in her saddle to follow his gaze.

But she saw nothing except a whitish cloud of dust. Then, a moment later, dark horses appeared against the white, and three riders rode toward them. Roark's hand went cautiously toward his Colt.

"You were right about Spafford Hall seeing your

112

father. I just talked with him."

"You mean my father's here?" she cried.

"He left several days ago."

Before she could reply, the men on horseback rode up. They were dusty and soiled, with unkempt beards and carrying rifles.

Samuel rode toward them, his black knee length coat flapping.

"Afternoon," he said. "The name's Samuel, servant of the Lord. Who be you gents?"

The eyes of the men passed him to skim over Jade, then fixed on Roark Montgomery.

"Name's Smith," the spokesman said dryly, a hint of the absurd in his voice. "This here's Jones, and this here," he said, gesturing his head toward a young man stroking his rifle, "is Brown."

"Brown" laughed, a high-pitched, hysterical sound, and Jade stiffened, a feeling of evil enveloping her.

Samuel ignored the response. "What do you want, boys?"

"Just thought to be neighborly. Wanted to warn you of trouble ahead. Piutes may soon be putting on some war paint."

"How do you know this?" Samuel asked.

Jade saw the men's eyes glancing toward Roark's gun hand, and Roark's steady gaze.

The spokesman, a man with reddish stubble, spat tobacco juice on the blowing dust, ignoring Samuel even though he was talking to him.

"Saw a man die passing through there a few weeks ago. Piutes got him."

"Sure it was Piutes?" asked Samuel.

"Reckon it weren't nobody else, Preacher. If'n I was

you—especially with a woman—I wouldn't be crossin' that route. The man's buried out there. Didn't have much time to make him a decent marker, did we boys?"

"Makes ya wanna cry. No good words spoken over him neither," said the other.

"Think it would've done him any good?" Roark asked smoothly.

Smith's eyes turned cold. "Ev'ry man ought to have words spoken over him."

"Seems to me," said Roark easily, "that a man in your position might prove himself wiser if he did his hearing while alive. He could do something about it then."

"Looks like we got us two preachers, boys. Only one sports a Colt and a Winchester."

"And a badge," said Roark, moving his jacket open just enough to show it. "I see you three aren't surprised."

"No reason to be. Ol' Spafford told us a lawman's been hanging around. You lookin' for silver or a scalp to hang on your belt?"

Jade tensed.

"Don't try it," Roark said as "Jones" reached toward his gun. "A few weeks ago two brothers were gunned down in Virginia City for trying something as foolish. Maybe you know them?"

"Why should I know 'em?" he said angrily.

"Just thought you might. Ramos brothers sound familiar?"

He glared, started to say something, then looked at the redhead, who calmly spat again.

"Never heard of no Ramos brothers. We just came in

114

from Salt Lake. Ask Spafford. Buried that man named Thomas O'Neil. Maybe you heard of him?"

Jade gasped, and the men seemed aware of her for the first time.

"You know him, miss?"

Jade didn't speak, just gripped the reins more tightly. She knew Roark couldn't take his eyes off the three, and she mustn't distract him.

"Thomas was her Pa," said Samuel. "He was my brother."

"Now ain't this wretched news. And to think we went and busted it on you careless like this. You please accept our sympathy, Miss O'Neil. Your Pa was a fine, upstandin' man."

"Best Christian I ever done seen. Ain't that so, boys?"

"Prayed ev'ry night. Readin' them words, preaching at us over the campfire. A man who's done gone to his final reward. So don't you cry none. It so happens before he died, shot full of arrows, he gave us this here token. But seein' how you're his daughter and all, he would've wanted you to have it." His eyes shifted to Roark. "I'm gonna reach into my shirt pocket, if it's alright with you, lawman."

The man produced a little black book and held it up so Roark could see it.

Samuel stared at the Bible.

"Hand it to me," he said hoarsely.

Moving his horse forward, Smith passed over the small book. "If you folks intend to go on toward Piute country, better be careful. Afternoon."

The three men rode off in the direction of Spafford's Station.

"This is Tommy's Bible, all right, but they're lying," said Samuel.

"Of course they were," said Roark. "They were paid."

"Then the only reason why they'd lie is to deceive Roark," said Jade.

"That's right, lass. If they can convince him that Tommy's been done in by the Piutes, Montgomery has no reason to remain in Virginia town. He'd return to California, and they'd be free to carry on with the diggings out at Seven-Mile."

"Pa doesn't even care if we think he's been killed!" said Jade.

"Not necessarily," said Roark. "He doesn't know you're here. He probably feels that Samuel can handle it well enough. I'm afraid it was a story meant for me."

Jade grew mute. Her spirits, high at coming on the adventure to sketch Samuel's pow-wow, tumbled.

"Well, I don't think we need to go looking for any marker for Thomas," said Samuel dryly.

Suddenly, Roark's gaze across the desert riveted toward the outer rim of the Utah mountains. "It doesn't appear as if Winnemucca is too interested in your pow-wow, Samuel."

Samuel turned and followed his gaze into the distance. One lone Indian sat watching them from the back of a skinny, spotted horse.

"I'll ride ahead and see what's up," Samuel said. As Jade watched him ride away, accompanied by the wind moaning through the hills, Roark asked her quietly, "Are you all right?"

"Oh, Roark, maybe you're right about my father.

116

Maybe he did shoot that man in San Francisco. And the other night when we came out of the International Hotel, maybe—"

"Don't think about it now. You've come to get a sketch, and I intend to see you get it—maybe not Winnemucca," he said with a smile, "but a Piute, just the same."

Samuel returned a few minutes later, his face sober.

"Trouble?" said Roark.

"Some man died out there, filled full of arrows, but it wasn't Thomas. The braves are spooked. The meeting with Winnemucca has been called off."

Roark turned to Jade. "I'd say Samuel's stalwart friend seated on his pony is every inch as worthy of your pencil and paper as Old Winnemucca. What do you say, Samuel? Think you can get him to pose with you?"

Samuel rubbed his beard and sniffed. "What do you have to pay him with?"

Jade made a vain attempt to sort through her satchel, but found nothing.

Roark produced a gold coin. "I'm sure the sketch will be worth every penny," he said to Samuel.

In a few minutes her easel was set up and Samuel and the Indian faced each other astride their horses. Samuel had a Bible in his hand and was reading, as the stalwart warrior listened, arms folded across his broad chest.

Jade was frowning. "This isn't exactly what I had in mind, Roark."

Roark was sprawled comfortably across some rocks, his hat pulled low to keep the sun and wind out of his eyes, watching her sketch, yet keeping an eye out for unwanted company.

"Did Beau ever tell you he was in love with you?"

Overcome by the unexpected question, she stammered, "B-Beau?"

"You do remember the man who devastated your life?"

"Oh. Him." She ignored the veiled sarcasm. "As a matter of fact, no."

He raised a brow. "I would think Beau would have loved you deeply."

Deeply. . .Jade liked the way the word came out. Her breath seemed to pause. Her heart contemplated not Beau loving her deeply, but what it would like to have Roark love her that way. She glanced sideways. Her voice was deliberately nonchalant. "Oh? Why would you think so?"

"I can think of many reasons. . .you are very fair to look at. You're a woman who loves the Lord, is virtuous, and is worthy of a man's devotion. And, you can be very charming."

Jade didn't dare look at him. She pretended to be busy sketching, but her heart was pounding and she felt her skin growing warm.

"How is it you were engaged to be married? A man should love a woman if he wants to marry her."

She was surprised at how calm her voice was. "The marriage had been planned for years. We grew up together. We used to play along the Mississippi riverbank, and, well—watch the boats paddle up and down."

"Enchanting."

She couldn't tell by his voice if he was serious or sarcastic, and she refused to take her eyes from her work. "We sort of took love for granted."

"I've heard of couples taking love for granted after twenty years of marriage, but before you even say your vows?"

Jade didn't know how to answer. She supposed there wasn't an answer that would satisfy him.

"Why do you want to know?"

"Curious."

The answer was too vague. She wanted to know more of what he thought. "Strange. . .I never thought of you as a curious man."

There were a few minutes of silence. Then, "Were you in love with Beau?"

"I never told him so."

"My dear, you're not serious!"

She was and felt his eyes studying her, but she couldn't find words to answer him.

"I'd never settle for that from a woman. Don't you think when a man and woman are in love, they ought to know it?"

"I'd rather not talk about Beau."

"Because it hurts too much to lose him, or because of the circumstances around the broken engagement?"

Jade tried to swallow and realized how dry her throat was. Feeling his gaze, she blurted out, "What of you? Have you ever been in love? Someone in San Francisco, perhaps?"

"No."

"Somehow I thought that half a dozen women would have their eye on you."

He smiled. "I said that I wasn't in love with anyone in

San Francisco. I didn't say there weren't any Christian women who would marry me."

"Sounds to me like you're hard to please, Mr. Montgomery."

"Oh, I am."

Hard to please. . .he would certainly have no interest in a frail young thing in Washoe who was losing weight. But he *had* said she was very fair. . . .

"You see, I happen to be very particular about the one woman I want."

Her hand tightened too much on the pencil. The line came stiff and hard. She erased it.

"Am I disturbing you?"

"Why would you think that?"

"No reason I suppose. Just thought I might."

"Well, I hope you find the *particular* woman you're looking for, Mr. Montgomery. Someday I'll sketch her for you."

His brow went up. "What do you think she'd be like?"

"She would be healthy, of course," Jade stated, wondering at herself for being so blunt, even while feeling irritated. "Strong, capable, mature, a woman of fine Christian character, someone who knows how to handle any situation that may arise."

"A strong, healthy woman has always been my first priority."

She gritted her teeth.

"She'll be expected to do all the labor," said Roark, his eyes glinting. "Up before dawn both winter and summer to get the fire going. She'll need to chop the wood, too. I don't care to fool with such things. Fix my breakfast, rub my horse down, do the laundry, then another seven hours of placer mining. Of course, anything she gets out of her rocker will be turned over to me; she might decide to spend it on something foolish—like a new dress."

Her eyes were a dark emerald and smoldering as they met his. "Maybe you can make a deal with the Piutes. I hear Indians treat their wives like slaves, too."

"I have several more gold coins. You don't think my expectations are unrealistic?" he asked innocently.

She finished the sketch at once and called, "Okay, Samuel, I'm done."

"It's about time, lass! Hey, Montgomery, you owe *me* a gold coin for putting up with all this posing."

Jade gathered her things together, each gesture one of irritation. She knew Roark had been teasing, and yet it irked her. He reached to carry her satchel.

"I'll carry it myself, Mr. Montgomery. Thank you."

Jade was already in the saddle, refusing to look at him when he walked up and untied his horse from the shrub. She snapped the reins in her hand, still irritated. Only reluctantly did she meet his gaze.

Roark rested his hands across the saddle and stood looking at her with a slight smile.

"Mr. Montgomery. . .I've been thinking. . .a Piute might not be tolerated well in Virginia City. Not if some skirmish breaks out with Winnemucca." Her eyes gleamed. "So, I've just the woman for you."

"I'm pleased to hear that. Is she healthy?"

"Oh very, far as I can tell. You know Eilley Orrum? She does a good deal of the miners' washing and cooking."

"Heard about it."

121

"She's as sturdy as a mule, even crossed the Forty-Mile Desert with her first husband—or was it her second? I forgot. But I'm sure she'll meet all your expectations."

"Does she have green eyes? I won't even consider it unless she does. I forgot to mention that. Green eyes are a must."

She felt a hot flush steal up her cheeks. "That narrows your list considerably."

"So it does. I told you, I am very particular when it comes to the one woman I want."

Chapter 10

As the days passed, illness broke out among the miners. Jade found herself too busy nursing the dying and aiding Samuel to think of Roark or her father.

"It's the water. Few can drink that stuff and live," Samuel told her.

The Washoe water with its strong arsenic content also had heavy traces of gold and silver. When taken in quantity, it doubled a man over with hideous cramps and intestinal disorder.

Samuel labored day and night, offering words of salvation and hope, and Jade stayed at his elbow, even though her strength was quickly exhausted.

It came as a surprise to her when Della, the girl Jade called "the girl with the rifle," pressed her way through the tent to clutch her arm. She had recently begun slipping into the women's Bible class that Jade had started, but she had made no profession of believing what she heard.

"It's my Pa," she whispered to Jade, her voice stern but shaking. "He's got himself real sick."

"I'll see Dr. McMannis about drugs. Dave Wylet just came in with supplies from Downieville. Where's your father now?"

"He's in the dugout, but it's not the water. He wasn't going to get himself sick on it, so he's been drinking almost straight stuff for the last week, adding just a little water."

Jade tried to look calm, but inside she wondered, *What can I do?* "I'll tell Dr. McMannis."

"I already did," Della said dully. "He said there's nothing he can do for him. I want you to talk to my father."

"If he's been drinking too much, it won't do any good to speak to him about the Lord now, Della. He won't understand."

Della's black eyes turned hard. "You said your God was love. Yet you won't come?"

Stung, Jade turned and grabbed her hooded cloak. "I'll tell Holly where I'm going."

In the small hovel that Della called home, there was an Indian blanket on the swept earth, and in one corner, a bed of dried branches covered with more blankets. The hovel reeked with stale whiskey, and it was all Jade could do to keep from gagging. How Della endured the miserable existence with her father, she couldn't imagine. By now, she would have expected the girl to have run away. There were several Indian pieces about, and Jade wondered where Della had gotten them.

"My mother was a Piute," she announced flatly, reading Jade's expression.

124

"Your mother, is she—"

"Dead."

"Garth's your only family?"

"I have an uncle with the tribe."

"Do you ever see him?"

Della's black eyes narrowed slightly as if judging the sincerity of her interest.

"Don't tell my father, but I ride out there often. I am received with scowls, but that does not bother me. The scowls are not so loud as they used to be. Now they expect to see me. If something happens to him, I am going back to my mother's people."

Feeling that the girl would undoubtedly be better off with the Indians than among the gamblers and drinkers, Jade said, "I think you should, Della. Get married; perhaps have a family. There's nothing for you here, unless you hope to marry a miner or discover your own bonanza. I would also urge you not to strive for riches, but to know as much about Jesus as you can."

"I have listened to your words in the women's meeting. I think about them."

Della gestured toward her mumbling father. "I keep asking him to listen, too, but he keeps telling me to shut up."

"You must keep listening and as long as he lives, there is hope for your father."

Della nodded. "Your Pa is like mine. They both face a dark passage that narrows."

Jade was silent. *A dark passage that narrows. . .and when they come to its end? What will they do without the Light of the World?* For a moment Jade was so distraught with thoughts of her own father that she hardly noticed Garth.

125

"We share the same sorrow," Della added just as Garth screamed and began to flail about as if fighting off some assailant. He was sweating profusely, and the odor coming from his unwashed body made Jade nauseous.

Between the two of them they wiped him with rags, and Jade tried to soothe him, but even in his condition he was too strong for her. Aware of how weak she was, she had to let Della hold him down.

"Pa! Be still! I've brought Jade to talk to you!"

"It's after me I tell you! Get it off me!"

For a moment Jade thought he was sober, and actually looked down at his blanket to see what could be disturbing him. But when Della held the candle close, his eyes were glassy, and there was nothing on the blanket.

"He thinks he sees monsters," Della explained. "Everything from spiders to evil spirits."

Jade looked at her in horror. Della's expression was immobile. "The doctor says he's hallucinating. It's all the bad stuff he poured down him."

Jade laid a hand on his shoulder and leaned toward him, reeling from the smell of whiskey. Certain he wouldn't understand a word she was saying, she nevertheless had to try.

"Garth?" Jade whispered, and wondered that even her voice sounded weak. "Garth, the love of God reaches out to you even in this moment. He has the power to set you free from the chains of sin. He's the only One who can."

There was silence.

"Can he hear you?" whispered Della.

"I don't know. . . .Garth? The Lord is merciful. He takes no pleasure in the death of those who reject Him.

Even on the cross He forgave those who crucified Him! He'll forgive you, too, if you'll accept Christ as your Saviour."

He shuddered and grumbled; his body shook violently.

Jade felt ill, and dizziness assailed her. Her own father was as bad off as Garth. Who would help him? Would he even accept help?

It is never so dark that God cannot deliver, never so late that He cannot save—she encouraged herself.

Outside, the wind moaned about the cabin. Della held the candle toward her shaking father. Aware that Della was staring at her, Jade went on, quoting Isaiah 1:18.

"Come now, and let us reason together, saith the Lord: though your sins be as scarlet, they shall be as white as snow; though they be red like crimson, they shall be as wool."

Garth moaned loudly and began flailing his arms, "Get out of here! Get away from me!"

Too late, she thought, and pain struck her heart as she grieved once more, picturing not Garth but Thomas O'Neil. She struggled to keep back the moisture welling up in her eyes. *Too late.*

"Does he hear?" Della whispered.

Jade didn't know, and wondered why the girl's frantic voice seemed so far away. She felt too ill to go on.

"Pray for him," Della urged.

Jade felt the girl's strong fingers digging into her arm, but everything was whirling about her in a hopeless state of dark confusion. The reality of death without the Saviour gripped Jade's heart as it never had before. Whether it was a man like Garth, a hopeless drunk, or a rich and powerful silver king, both would pass through the gates of death alone and empty-handed. She shuddered and suddenly her own relationship with the Lord became more precious. She, too, was ill, yet she had a Saviour to bear her through the doorway into eternity. She wouldn't go alone.

Garth shouted loudly, his voice shaking Jade out of her silence. The sound reminded her of a wounded animal as his arms struck out wildly, smashing the candle from Della's hand.

"Get it off me!" he bellowed.

The cabin sank into shadows except where the embers glowed red in the stove. Della wrestled to hold her father down.

Overcome with dizziness, Jade's brain was reeling as she smelled something, "Della!" she cried weakly.

The blanket had caught a spark, smoldering, and now the dry brush beneath the scorched spot gave way and began to smoke.

Garth was delirious. Yelling at Della, he clutched a fistful of her dark hair and refused to let go.

Jade tried to smother the sparks with the blanket, but the dry pine needles where like an old Christmas tree. Her lungs burned from the fumes, and she collapsed helplessly into coughing spasms.

Della struck her father in desperation and broke free, grabbing the blanket to smother the flame. She quickly put it out, but the smoke left Jade in a helpless huddle on the floor, choking.

Della ran to the door and flung it open, allowing a gust of wind to hurl snow flakes into the dugout.

"Della!" a voice shouted from outside in the darkness. "Is Jade here?"

"Mr. Montgomery! Quick!"

Roark's dark silhouette appeared in the doorway. Bending over, Roark lifted Jade from the floor and held her while the agony continued. When the coughing quieted, he wrapped her in the blanket Della gave him, and carried her to his horse. On the ride back to the O'Neils' cabin, Jade hovered close to unconsciousness. The freezing gusts of wind whipped at them, and now and then, she was aware of Roark's strong arms supporting her in the saddle.

Snow continued to fall throughout the following day and night, and the Washoe winds howled like an angry tyrant about the cabin.

It was the second day after Roark had brought Jade home. He stepped out of her room, removing the cloth tied about his face. He paused when he saw Shaun standing in the shadows clutching Keeper, and quivering with anxiety.

"Son, you're not to be in the cabin now. You're to stay at Samuel's."

"Is—is Jade going to die?"

Roark found Shaun's drawn face as heart-rending as the sight of Jade, pale and thin.

"I don't want Jade to die like Mama did," Shaun gasped, choking with emotion.

Roark caught the small boy up into his arms and held him close as he walked to the fire glowing in the stove. Shaun's thin arms clutched his neck tightly and he wept, his body shaking with sobs as Roark soothed him.

From the bedroom, Jade could barely hear their voices. They echoed in her ears like distant calls she couldn't answer. Her eyes were blurred, and the room was unsteady each time she tried to sit up. Her feverish mind groped for answers as a small yellow light burned on the barrel beside her bed.

Where was she? Home. . .yes. . .St. Louis. . .She tried to call her mother. Where was she? She couldn't concentrate for long; she was too tired. Her lungs burned, yet she felt no fear; peace seemed to envelop her like a warm blanket, even as the persistent cough came to claim what strength she had.

Jade's agony brought Roark into the bedroom. She was trying to sit up, gasping weakly.

She felt arms embracing her, but they didn't belong to her mother—or to Holly. Her mind thought of Shaun, but it was a man's voice speaking into her ear. Beau? No. It was different. He was holding her up in a sitting position, holding her with hands that didn't shake, not even when he wiped the blood from her mouth. . . .Roark. . .Fear and dread ebbed as she clutched at him weakly, hearing his reassuring voice, and responding to the security of his touch. The coughing spasm darkened her mind until it began to recede into a faint, but this time the faint didn't come. She was still awake, and she thought he was praying, yet sometimes it seemed that he was talking to her, too. She couldn't quite make out what he was saying, but she didn't need to. Her wordless prayer ascended with his, and at that moment, Jade knew she loved him. The realization came naturally and sweetly. She tried to say the words aloud, but the strength wasn't there.

Calm flowed through her soul and slowly her body grew less rigid with pain and anxiety. Feeling his nearness, comforted by his hand soothing her damp hair, a heavy sleep claimed her mind, and the darkness was welcomed.

On and off through an uncertain passage of time, she recognized the voice of her Uncle Samuel praying beside her bed.

A vision of a warm, sunny morning in St. Louis filled her mind. She was all dressed up in green satin, and she and Roark were going to church. They were laughing and talking of marriage. Then suddenly she was lost in a blinding snowstorm, so ill she couldn't walk. Stumbling into a ditch, she lay shuddering and coughing herself senseless. And Roark wasn't there. . . . He had married someone else and was serving God among the Indians—

Her eyes fluttered open to face the weak afternoon light peeking through the bedroom window. Fully awake for the first time, Jade lay very still. Her eyes glanced about the room, but she was alone.

In the next room she recognized the voices of Samuel and Roark. Reality returned with a rush. How many days had she been in bed? A week? A month? She touched her face and found her hair in two thick braids. Dazed, she felt her body beneath the blankets. Thin! Terribly so! With despair she realized that Roark was seeing her in her most wretched condition. Romance, if there had been any, was certainly dead.

In a moment of unguarded emotion she started to cry. Then she forced the tears back. She knew she wouldn't be able to stop if she gave in to them.

Slowly, with difficulty, she raised herself on one elbow and turned toward the mirror. Her eyes saw a thin, fragile girl looking back at her. A choked sob died in her throat, and she fell back against the pillow.

"Oh, dear Lord, no. . ."

She stiffened as she heard someone enter the small

131

room. She knew it was Roark, even before he spoke. Quickly she tried to hide the evidence of tears, but nothing seemed to escape him.

"May I sit down?" His voice was calm.

Almost like a doctor, she thought dully.

"I'd rather be alone," she murmured.

He sat down anyway and reached for her hand. She clenched it weakly into a balled fist, but if he noticed, he pretended that he didn't.

She tried not to enjoy his touch. She told herself his attitude was only that of a doctor ministering to a frail little girl in need of healing.

"Garth is dead—" she whispered weakly. "I heard you tell Samuel."

"He died in his sleep a few days ago."

"I don't suppose anything I said did him any good?"

"No one knows that except God. Yet, Garth had time to turn to the Lord if he wanted to. You're a rare lady Jade. Not many would even try like you did."

Jade lowered her head. Sick in body and spiritually despondent, it was easy to slip into feelings of pity. "What good am I to God or anyone else lying here too sick to do anything but have people waiting on me!"

She saw eyes search her face, and his dark brows went up. "Not growing bitter on me, are you?" he whispered.

She turned her head away.

"Look at me, Jade," he said, and his voice was quiet. She turned tormented eyes to his face and saw subdued concern there.

"What is it, honey? You can tell me."

Yes. She could tell Roark; she could tell him her

132

deepest feelings. Yet, there was something she couldn't tell him—she couldn't tell him she was in love with him, hopelessly so. Instead, she said, "Oh, Roark, I'm so afraid."

"Afraid?" He squeezed her hand and smiled. "A young lady willing to face Winnemucca and old Garth, afraid?"

"I'm afraid of weakness, of being helpless. My health is gone! What else is there? Nothing makes any sense to me."

"Don't you suppose there's wisdom behind the trials God allows to come your way?"

"Oh yes, Roark, only sometimes I'm afraid they just happen."

"No, honey, God's plans are never haphazard. Each experience is weighed and measured to accomplish a purpose."

"Oh, Roark, you're not just saying that to make me feel better?"

"Jade, you know me better than that!"

"Well—"

"You're sick and weary, Jade, that's why you're so discouraged right now. But you're getting better. In a few more days you'll be smiling again. And when you are—"

"Do you really think so?"

"I do."

"But I'll never be able to serve the Lord the way I wanted to, and it's so frustrating. I feel hemmed in, even useless! And it's frightening."

"In your position, I might feel the same way. I'm sure I would. But are we to say what God finds worthwhile?"

"No, yet. . ."

133

"Is it your accomplishments that make you valuable to God?"

"No. . ."

"It's you He wants, Jade. Your life, your obedience, your love."

They were quiet for a moment.

"Feel better?" he finally asked with a smile.

"A little." She smiled weakly. "But shattered plans and dreams aren't easy to put back together."

"You're right. But if He is Lord, is He not then Master of our plans and service?"

Her eyes closed wearily. "You still don't think He ever wanted me to be a missionary among the Indians, do you?" she murmured tiredly.

"The way it looks now, no. You're an artist. A very good one."

Her eyes opened and a glimmer of light glinted in their green depths.

"In the spring, I'll take you to see my father, and when you're better, you can think about studying art. You'd enjoy it wouldn't you?"

"Very much, Roark. But I have five cents in my purse," she said weakly. "How can I pay your father? And I must support myself while I study art—"

His fingers crossed her lips. "One day at a time. Right now, it's enough for you to recover the strength to make the trip to San Francisco."

She smiled, contented now, and her eyes grew heavy and closed again.

I love you, she thought, and within a few minutes she was asleep.

Chapter 11

It was the week of Christmas. Jade was sitting up in bed, and Shaun was obediently holding the small hand mirror as she brushed and worked her curls into a semblance of feminine grace. She scowled. Why was it that being sick took the shine from hair? Well, it was the best she could do. She sighed and stared at her green eyes and thick lashes. At least they hadn't fallen out. She pinched her cheeks trying to put color into them. She heard Shaun smother a laugh.

"Come on, Jade, hurry. Roark don't care what you look like."

"Who said I'm trying to look nice for him?"

"You don't need to say it. I know. Besides, he's seen you at your worst, and he still comes around. No use worrying none."

She might have winced at that statement, but the more she thought about it, the more she realized what Shaun said was true, and it was comforting. Roark

Montgomery had definitely seen her at her very worst.

Things were hard, but she was alive, and she rejoiced in that gift as well as the expected trip to San Francisco in the spring to visit Dr. Montgomery.

"He's here now!" At the sound of a deep male voice, Shaun dropped the mirror on the bed and ran out.

The voice of Dave Wylet joined with Roark's as they entered, stamping snow off their feet. Holly and Uncle Samuel joined them, and for a moment Jade heard the rise and fall of voices and laughter, as the shouts of "Merry Christmas" rang out.

"Look, a present! Wrapped in paper, even!" cried Shaun. "With my name!"

"Roark, how on earth did you come up with wrapping paper?" cried Holly.

"You can ask Dave about that."

Jade settled herself as nicely as she could against the back of the bed, and touched her hair again as she heard steps. She looked up and smiled as Roark came through the door. He was the image of masculine strength, and her heart gave an odd little lurch at seeing him again. He had been gone for almost three weeks.

"Merry Christmas, Roark," she murmured.

His eyes locked with hers. "It is now."

He walked up and sat on the barrel beside the bed.

"I'm sorry I don't have a present for you. Especially after all you've done for me the last six weeks."

"Emerald eyes and ebony curls, what more could a man ask for on Christmas morning?"

"You're kind to say so. But I look terrible, and we

both know it. I've lost so much weight the wind would blow me away."

His eyes contradicted her words as he handed her a package. "Maybe this will help."

She opened it and discovered a fur-lined hooded cloak. "Roark! How did you ever manage!"

"Dave brought it over on his last trip. It's not exactly what I had in mind for such an attractive young lady, but it will keep you warm. We'll save style for San Francisco."

"I think it's beautiful!"

He reached into his jacket and handed her an envelope. "I have one more gift for you."

She smiled and tore the letter open. It was dated December 25th and signed. She read the promise that he had written.

Her eyes met his and gleamed like emerald fire. "*Anything* I want in San Francisco?" she teased cautiously. "Aren't you afraid I'll take advantage of you?"

"Anything," he stated. "And you can take advantage of me anytime you want."

To cover her embarrassment, she hastened, "I shall have the finest dinner on the wharf, and then a carriage ride along the Bay."

"It's probably best if you don't talk of San Francisco cuisine now," he jested. "Looks like salted mule is going to be the staple of Washoe until spring."

"No. Is it really that bad, Roark?"

"It is. Not that I want to dishearten such a pretty face today, but I've always thought a woman ought to know what she's in for. Besides, I think you can handle it."

Jade squirmed a little at the thought of more trouble.

137

She knew food and wood were scarce; Holly had told her that. But she hadn't thought it was that desperate.

"How bad is it?"

"Sugar was sold out last week. No more chocolates." He smiled slightly, his eyes teasing her.

"I'll manage," she said with a rueful smile, thinking of the boxes he had regularly bought her.

"How about eighty dollars a sack for vermin infested flour?"

She gasped. Eighty dollars! Who among them had so much money? Certainly not Samuel. And she and Holly were penniless still.

"Not that there's much flour to buy," he added.

"Any word from Carson?"

"Messengers were dispatched a few days ago. Word's arrived that the valley is snowbound—the inhabitants slowly starving."

"Can't the pack animals bring in food from Placerville?"

"Afraid not. The drifts are sixty feet high in places, and there's no let up in the storms. It wouldn't be so bad if we could hunt game, but the animals know better than to get trapped on the peaks in winter. But enough gloomy talk. It's Christmas, and Dave and I managed to get a nice, fat 'bird' for Holly to bake. I'll carry you into the kitchen to see this marvelous sight."

She saw the glint of humor, and at once grew suspicious. She narrowed her lashes. "What kind of a Christmas bird?" she asked cautiously.

"Oh. . .a nice, plump fellow."

Roark walked to the door and called smoothly, "Samuel, do you have that Christmas 'goose' plucked yet?"

"He's still trying to get the feathers off," came Wylet's innocent reply.

"Still *trying?*" Jade said. "You mean they—they don't want to come off?"

"Stubborn goose."

"It's not a goose! What is it, Roark! Oh—it couldn't be a—a—?"

"Jade, I'm disappointed. Where's your confidence in Dave and me? You couldn't find two better hunters in all of Washoe."

She smiled in spite of herself. "If things are as bad as you say, and going to get worse, then Holly and I had better show more appreciation."

"I'm glad you see it that way. No questions asked?"

"Well. . .no, you know what they say about looking a gift mule in the mouth."

He laughed and walked back to the bed. "It's time you sat by the fire. Feel up to it?"

"I—I think so."

"Don't get up. I'll carry you."

Late that night when Jade awoke from a sound sleep, she realized something that took her by surprise. They had all spent a wonderful Christmas day together, and neither she nor anyone else had asked Roark about Thomas O'Neil. No one had heard from him, and, indeed, her father had not even crossed her mind. She prayed for him and for Roark, then let sleep claim her again.

The long wintry nights passed in flickering candle light. Along the Six-Mile Canyon, some strained their ears hopelessly for the familiar tinkle of the bells of a pack mule train, but only the icy wind greeted them.

Washoe was abandoned for the winter.

"The situation in Virginia City is growing worse," Holly told her one day in late March. "We're truly indebted to the clever abilities of Roark and Dave in providing food and wood, but I'm not sure how much longer even they can find food."

Just then, Shaun came tearing into the cabin. "Mule train!"

Jade and Holly snatched their cloaks from the pegs and headed into town after Shaun. Men were coming from everywhere like ants. The word had spread quickly. "Mule train!"

There was not a sweeter sound to any ear than the clattering hooves and the tinkle of bells. Everywhere Jade and Holly heard, "Mule train! Hear them bells?"

The miners were hollering with delight, tossing their battered hats into the air.

And sure enough, as the girls reached the main street, they saw mules heavily loaded down with barrels and packs. Hungry miners tore open the first barrel—and the cry that expected life-saving bacon or flour died with a disappointed groan.

"Why, this here ain't nothing but whiskey!"

The owner from San Francisco scowled. "*Just* whiskey?! Why last week I turned down $8,000 cash for this load!"

Ignoring him, another miner ran to the next mule and opened a barrel—the next, and the next—

The men looked at each other in despair—70 gallons of assorted alcohol! One old man sat down and wept. Groaning, the men began to tear at the other barrels. Tobacco, drinking glasses, plates—

"What's the matter with you? What'd ya take us fer

up here, a bunch o' drinkin' scum?"

The driver, intending to go into business for himself, was speechless. He watched the men turn away, their stomachs growling with hungry disappointment.

Shaun's mouth was open as he looked up at Jade, who had watched it all in stunned silence. Finally, she drew him away, and they started the slow walk back up the hill with Holly.

"Hey, Miss, isn't this Virginia City?" the driver called to her.

"It is, mister. But that's the only thing you've got right."

However, two long weeks later, a second mule train arrived bringing a load of flour. "They held an auction," Holly told Jade, who had stayed at the cabin this time. "A man paid five dollars a pound for it."

"Then I saw him mixing it with snow and eating it right there!" said Shaun.

"We need to be very thankful. It's only the grace of the Lord that has helped us stay alive," said Jade.

Somehow they struggled through the long winter. The short days and long nights took their toll, but Dave, Roark, and Samuel managed to keep food on the table and wood in the stove. Not even Keeper went too hungry; even though Jade knew Shaun was feeding him from his own small portion, she said nothing.

Finally, spring arrived, and the snow around the cabin began to melt. Then two more pack trains made it in. With the fresh arrival of food and the promise of a prosperous summer, Sun Mountain came alive again, emerging from its winter cocoon. It didn't take long for the men to forget the hardships of the long winter. The taverns filled, the cards were shuffled, the dice rolled, and once again bullets flew.

One afternoon Holly stood staring at the letter delivered to her by Pony Express.

"I don't believe it, but it's finally come."

"What has?" Jade asked.

"An invitation from Aunt Norma."

Holly looked at Jade, shocked. "It seems she wants us to come and live with her in New York City—all three of us."

"Well," said Jade, reaching for the letter, "this is what you've been waiting for."

Holly blushed and turned away, busying herself at the table.

"Aren't you going to write and tell her that you and Shaun are coming?"

"Not me!" cried Shaun. "I'm staying with Uncle Samuel, even if Pa never comes home. I'm going to learn to be a preacher."

Holly fumbled with the pots and pans. "I—I can't go now."

Jade was enjoying herself. "No? Why on earth not, Holly? You might meet a New York lawyer at one of those fine balls, remember? Think what that will mean. Money, pretty clothes—a whole closet full of them! Balls every night—"

Holly interrupted. "I can't go. . .now. . .that is—I don't want to leave."

"No?" asked Jade innocently. "But, Holly! Think of that nice, fine house!"

Holly turned her head and smiled at her sister. "All right, Jade O'Neil, don't keep rubbing in the salt."

Jade laughed at her.

"I won't be going anywhere until Dave decides it's time," said Holly, so softly that Jade had to strain her ears.

"Until *Dave* decides?" Jade asked in amusement. "My, how sweet and submissive we're becoming."

Holly turned, her face flushed. She tied and untied her apron.

"Dave wants to wait awhile and then go to Sacramento. He says Virginia City is going to boom for the next few years. He expects some big silver discoveries. Everyone thinks the Comstock Lode is the richest one of all. People will be flocking here, and between us, we'll make enough money to buy some land to raise horses on."

Holly drew in a breath. "I didn't tell you yet, Jade, not with the uncertaintly going on about you and Pa and everything—but," she smiled suddenly and threw up her hands, "he asked me to marry him. I said yes."

"Wonderful! Why didn't you tell me!"

"You were too sick. It was just after Christmas. I didn't want to jump ahead to happiness when we didn't know how it was going to turn out with you—well, you know."

Jade laughed and threw her arms around her. "I'm glad, Holly. When?"

"This summer. We're going to ask Samuel to marry us as soon as the little church building goes up. Dave's bringing back a load of materials for decoration."

"Married," breathed Shaun, who looked at Jade with veiled sympathy. "What about you, Jade? You're prettier than Holly. You going to marry Raork?"

"Shaun!" said Holly, hands on hips in mock indignation. "That's a fine compliment to pay me!"

He looked sheepish and, to cover it, glanced again at Jade. "Are you and—"

"Shaun, let's just be happy for Holly and Dave. I

143

don't want to spoil it by discussing me. All right?" She turned to Holly. "You'd better sit down and write Norma that you're not coming."

Holly nodded and went for pencil and paper. Shaun scooped up Keeper and stood beside Jade.

"I'll look after you when I grow up, Jade. You don't need to worry."

His brotherly concern was touching. Jade smiled softly and took his chin her her hand. "The Lord will look after us both," she whispered, "and Keeper, too."

"Pa's in trouble, isn't he, Jade?"

At the abrupt and unexpected change in the conversation, she looked at him and wondered how he knew. Thomas O'Neil had been a subject that remained undiscussed.

If he knew enough to ask, Jade knew it was time to be truthful.

"Yes, I'm afraid he is. Who told you about Pa?"

"Uncle Samuel. Mr. Montgomery's gone to arrest Pa."

Stunned by his calm announcement, she stared down at the boy. "Shaun! Whatever do you mean!"

"Last night I was with Uncle Samuel and Roark. It was late, and I was supposed to be sleeping. A man rode in from William's Station."

William's Station, thought Jade anxiously. It was somewhere in Seven-Mile along the base of the mountain. She knew little else except that the Williams brothers ran it.

"The man gave Roark a message. It was from Pa."

"Shaun! Are you sure?"

"I heard Roark tell Uncle Samuel that Pa wanted to see them both. Roark said he was going to risk the meeting. After that, Roark went into town."

Her heart slammed in her chest. So that was why she hadn't seen Roark today! Why hadn't he told her? Anything could happen. Did he still think she wouldn't understand?

"I've decided I'm going to like Roark anyway. What about you, Jade?" he whispered. "You'll still like him, too, won't you? Even if he arrests Pa?"

"Is Samuel still here?"

"He was saddling the mule a few minutes ago."

Although weak, Jade ran in the direction of the stable to see Samuel mounting the mule, ready to ride.

"Samuel! Wait!" She ran up. "Shaun just told me about Pa. Can you trust the message? Suppose it's a trap? You saw those men we met at Spafford's! They may intend to kill Roark!"

Samuel's brows furrowed. "Just as I thought Shaun was asleep last night and was wrong, I'm sure of nothing, now. Neither is Montgomery, but Tommy's there, and he wants to talk, so Roark's willing to go."

Jade felt a stab of guilt. "This is my fault, Samuel, I've forced him into risking his life. Oh why didn't he tell me before he left?"

"What was he to say, lass? That he's riding off to arrest your father? As for risk—Roark does nothing he doesn't want to. You do some praying, not just for your Pa, but for Montgomery. It's one thing for me to face a trap knowingly in order to give Tommy another chance. It's another matter for a man like him. He's doing it for you, Jade. You understand that don't you?"

She could find no words as she reached up and grabbed his arm. When Samuel leaned forward, Jade kissed his bearded cheek, then watched him ride off.

Chapter 12

The shout came like wind down C Street. "Here comes the Pony Express! Make way!"

Jade grabbed Shaun's arm and pulled him back. Others also scrambled to get out of the street, but to everyone's disappointment, Pony Bob rode straight through Virginia City without stopping.

"Did you see him, Jade? Looked to me like he's bad injured! Do you think he was attacked by robbers?"

Jade tensed. Not robbers, but perhaps Indians. They looked up as a second horse came galloping toward them. This time the rider jumped off his horse onto the boardwalks.

"C'mon, Jade! Look! He stopped at Fargo's!"

The crowd ran to the Wells Fargo and Company's Express Office. When Jade caught up with Shaun, the man's mustang was foaming at the mouth and being swiftly led away to water and rest.

"I just came from Buckland's Station along the Carson River! The Piutes are coming!" shouted the expressman to the crowd.

Indians! Jade's breath stopped. She tried to push her way through the crowd.

"It can't be!" shouted one. "Why, just this winter we was buyin' brush from 'em, even a few goods!"

"Old Chief Winnemucca wouldn't attack Virginia town!" another shouted.

"The Piutes attacked William's Station yesterday!" cried the expressman.

"What! Attacked the Station?"

"Burned the place to the ground. Killed all that were there—men, women, and one child. Even done the dog in."

Jade's heart stopped. William's Station! That was where Roark and Samuel had ridden to meet her father!

Shaun's mouth opened, and he grabbed her arm, his fingers digging into her flesh. "William's Station! Indians—maybe thousands of 'em with arrows dipped in rattlesnake poison, tomahawks and rifles—"

"Hush, Shaun, listen!"

"How many of them?" shouted a man.

"Plenty, enough to outnumber us. They're riding up Six-Mile near Devil's Gate. Better arm yourselves while you can."

The men began to scatter, ignoring Jade. "Sound the word! We gotta get the boys out of the mines!"

The warning spread like fire; all work ceased. Jade grabbed Shaun's arm and started back to the cabin. Mules were being commandeered; men were rushing to buy the remaining ammunition, and sentries galloped off in the direction of Six- and Seven-Mile

Canyons to sound the alarm.

Hearing the ruckus as miners streamed past the O'Neils' cabin, Holly came out the door just as Jade and Shaun arrived. Shaun dropped Jade's hand and ran ahead, shouting, "Thousands of Piutes are riding up Six-Mile. There's been a massacre!"

"Indians!" wailed Holly. "Oh, Jade! And with the men gone!"

Jade tried to think clearly but she could hear the mountain buzzing with voices, and all she could think of was Roark and Samuel.

"Where was the attack?" asked Holly.

"William's Station."

Holly went pale. "Are you sure, Jade?"

"It was William's all right," a man called, hurrying past. "Whole place's smoking. Took some scalps, too."

Shaun gripped at Jade's skirt. "What about Uncle Samuel and Roark?"

She knelt and scooped his face into her cold hands, praying that she sounded calm. "Whatever happens, the Lord is with them—and with us. Let's not frighten ourselves into imagining more than we know. They left three days ago. Why, they may be on their way back now."

"Through Indian territory?" cried Holly. "You heard what they said—the Piutes are at Devil's Gate!"

"I don't see any Indians yet," said Jade. "You know how stories get started, Holly."

A group of men were walking toward town, and Holly cried out. "Are the Piutes really coming?"

"Looks that way, Miss Holly. Better get out of that cabin and into Samuel's dugout. That cabin'll catch fire too easy. Where's Samuel and Montgomery?"

149

Holly couldn't speak, and Jade's throat tightened as she forced out the words. "They rode to William's Station several days ago."

The men exchanged glances, then looked sheepish. "Well—maybe they got out in time. I wouldn't worry none about them two rawhides. They can handle themselves."

"You girls got a rifle?"

"No," Jade said.

"When them Injuns come creeping about looking for some black curls, you'll wish you did."

Jade tried not to gasp, but Holly did.

"Don't tell her that, you coyote! You wanna scare the girls to death?"

"Just warnin' them, that's all." The man strode downhill with his rifle across his arm.

"Don't pay him no mind. The men of Virginia town will protect their ladies, you can be sure of that."

Jade was sure of nothing. Shaun turned suddenly and ran toward Samuel's dugout.

"Shaun, come back here!"

"I gotta hide Keeper, Jade! The Indians will put an arrow in him like they did that dog!"

A group of men came walking up. "Who's in charge around here?" Jade called.

"No one, yet, Miss. There ain't no authority, and no garrison nearby. We're all forming a group now to discuss what to do. We're aiming to call on Bill Stewert."

"Stewert? He's not in town," she said. "He left yesterday, I think. He rode down Gold Canyon."

"Then what about his young partner? Name's Henry Meredith, I do believe," said one.

"Yup, a gallant man, Henry."

"Well," cried Jade, "isn't someone going to send a telegram to Governor Downey at Sacramento? He's sure to send men and arms."

"They done that already, Miss. There's plenty of men, but no weapons."

"What about Salt Lake?"

"Through Piute territory?" he queried as he moved on toward town. "It's hundreds of miles. No one could get through without getting scalped!"

By evening the assembly had gathered on B Street to hear Henry Meredith. Jade stood with Holly and Shaun as his voice rang out.

"I want a candle or lantern burning in every tent and cabin tonight," Meredith shouted. "Let no man remove his clothes. If you go to bed, go with your boots on and your weapon at your side, and have rations in your pockets. Be ready at a moment's notice."

"What about our womenfolk?" someone called out.

"We'll take them to Peter O'Riley's."

O'Riley's stone hotel was not completed, but the walls were partially up. "It's now Fort Riley," said Shaun proudly as they moved in with the others. "Look, Jade, guards are on sentry to protect us."

"Thank goodness," said Holly.

Throughout the long night, Jade couldn't sleep, and got up frequently to look out the open window. Even though the gambling halls were open, the men had their guns ready, but no attack came. At dawn, she watched the men gather on C Street, then ride toward Gold Canyon on their way to William's Station. Her heart turned toward Roark and Samuel. Were they alive?

Chapter 13

I must talk to you, dear brother, Samuel. My path has led me into grave error. Your words have not been wasted. I'd like to make things right, but don't know how. If you would see me, come to William's Station. I will meet with Montgomery and hear what he has to say.

Tommy

Samuel and Roark sat on their horses a safe distance behind some trees near William's Station, re-reading the message that had brought them here. The morning was quiet and crisp with the murmur of the Carson River and the wind sweeping through the willows. It was too quiet, Roark told himself. The call of a mountain bluejay was interrupted by the foreboding appearance of a black object high in the sky. As the buzzard circled, Roark squinted, his eyes taking in the scene.

"Something's dead," he told Samuel.

Roark had been uneasy since leaving Virginia City. Was Thomas the kind of man who would reconsider his life in a time of distress? He wasn't sure, but something kept telling him that he wasn't.

He looked at Samuel from under his hat. Samuel's bushy dark brows were hunched.

Roark touched his Colt, easing it slightly. "What do you think?" he murmured.

"I don't like what I feel, lad. Let me ride in first. If anything's wrong, I'll know it straight off. Then you get yourself out of here fast."

Roark laid a hand on his arm. Samuel followed his gaze riveted on the barn door. It was slightly ajar.

"Someone's waiting in there," said Roark. "He could be friendly."

"Could be. But I'm inclined to believe he's got a rifle aimed at the first man who rides in wearing a badge."

Roark waited several more minutes, studying the situation. "Wait here, Samuel. That buzzard's interested in what's on the other side of that hill. I'll circle around there first and have a look. You stay out of sight."

Roark rode back to where a bend in the canyon led up into some split rocks. He could see what appeared to be an entrance to a cave located further up. He leaned over the side of his horse. There were footprints. Some were smaller, and he judged them to belong to a woman. Perhaps two.

Curious, he looked up at the cave and saw that the entrance was blocked. Was there someone inside?

He left his horse behind some trees and edged his way closer toward the path. As he rounded some rocks, he saw what interested the buzzard. A man lay face down in the dirt. There were several bullet holes in his back. Roark could tell he had been dead for some time. With his boot, he turned him over.

"Hello, Montgomery."

Roark turned slowly. A man stepped from behind the trees. He was in his mid-forties, tall, slim, handsome, with a shock of dark wavy hair and green eyes that were all too familiar. He was dressed well, with a white shirt and sleeve garters. Roark could recognize a gambler anywhere.

"Thomas." Roark glanced at the Winchester aimed at his chest.

"Easy, lawman. Nice and gentleman like—unbuckle your belt. One slight move toward that Colt, and you'll force me to shoot."

"I thought your letter to Samuel was a fake."

Thomas O'Neil flashed a smile. It was so much like Jade's that Roark felt a wince of pain.

"I know your reputation, Montgomery. They say you're better with that gun than Langford Peel or Eldorado Johnny."

Roark moved his hands toward his belt.

"Easy," breathed Thomas again. "Don't try anything."

"I didn't know I had a reputation. Am I to feel honored being compared to Langford Peel and Eldorado?"

Roark loosened his belt.

"Set it down slow like. . .that's it. Now, kick it aside and move toward the cave."

"Your friend?" Roark murmured dryly, nodding toward the dead man.

Thomas's arm relaxed just slightly. The quick smile

was friendly but empty.

"He was nobody to me."

"So I gather."

"He got in the way. Wouldn't behave. When a partner gets too restless, it's time to narrow the game."

"So you shot him in the back."

"What makes you think I did it? It might have been Jesse or Ernie. Right now they're keeping an eye on the Piutes. They're heading this way."

"Why would Piutes be headed for Williams'?"

"I'm afraid you and Samuel will be the only ones here to ask them that. Before they arrive, I'll be headed for Virginia City."

"So you intend to use Samuel for your selfish purposes again?"

"How righteous you sound, Montgomery. A pity. . . too bad you can't be tempted. Think what we might share in Virginia town. Why, with your gun you could take them all; together we could run the place. I'd run the gambling, and you'd run the town. We'd be sleeping in silver encrusted beds, with silver doorknobs on the doors, and have them all eating from our hand."

"I've never cared for cowards eating from my hand, nor for silver doorknobs."

"So it goes. . .so it ends here."

"Like him, in the back? You're a brave man, Thomas. I hope Shaun never knows just how brave."

Thomas blinked at the name. His cheek twitched, then he clamped his jaw tight. "Shut up! Leave Shaun out of this."

"He's in the middle of this. He's your son."

"I don't want to hear it!"

"Of course you don't. Responsibility demands unselfishness—and some honor. You've shed yours like a snake does its skin."

"Keep jabbing at me, and I won't wait for the Piutes to take your scalp. Samuel come?"

"Did you think he wouldn't?"

He smiled and shrugged. "Poor Sammy. . .I haven't been fair, using him like this. But that's the way it has to be. I had my doubts, actually. Not about him, but you. I thought you might see through the letter. With a letter like that, I knew Sammy would come. He can't help it. It's the preacher in him. He wants to convert me so bad, he'd cross the Forty-Mile on foot to do it."

"I'm glad I've met you face to face, Thomas. My opinion of you was correct. You'd sacrifice Samuel or anyone else for your own survival. You'll turn on anyone who gets in your way. The Ramos brothers, Jesse and Ernie—no wonder you never cared about your kids and wife."

"If you know so much, Montgomery, you weren't very smart in showing up. Why did you come?"

"Because of Jade."

The green eyes blinked. Roark saw the smile disappear. For a moment there was silence.

"She's in Virginia City. So're Holly and Shaun. Their mother died last year."

"Shut up. Just shut up."

"Jade believes in you. She believes you're innocent of the shooting in California. She's begged me to give you a chance to turn yourself in peaceably."

For a moment Thomas stared at him, then swept Roark with a soft laugh.

"Well, well. Between Samuel and Jade you've backed yourself into a corner, Montgomery. I almost

156

feel sorry for you. It's the same pressure I feel when Sammy gets going on me with those words. Too bad you risked your head for my daughter, though. Jade's wrong about me."

"I don't suppose her trust does anything to soften you up?"

"It's way past all that. If I gave myself up to you now, I'd hang. I don't love anyone enough to hang for them. Whatever the cost, I want to keep living. Sorry to disappoint you all. But I'm not the sentimental type to repent sudden-like and go to the gallows, just so everyone else can feel good about my last hours."

"I didn't expect you would. At least let Samuel live."

"I've no intention of shooting Sammy. What do you take me for? The Piutes will take care of that."

"Why would the Piutes attack Williams'?"

Thomas O'Neil gestured toward the cave. "Two Piute Indian squaws are in there.

"I had nothing to do with it. It was the Williams brothers. The fools lured them here." He glanced up toward the smoldering sun. "In about an hour from now the braves will sweep down on the station. I didn't plan this, Montgomery, it just worked out for me. Gambler's luck, I call it. I won't need to do anything but leave you here for the Piutes."

"You've got to warn Samuel."

Thomas said nothing. He gestured to the cave. "Get up there."

"If I don't? Why don't I just make you shoot me now? The shot will alarm Samuel."

"I know you, Montgomery. I can depend on your integrity." Thomas smiled qickly. "You might alert Sammy, it's true. You may even save him—but what of those two women in there? Make the slightest move, and I'll see they die, too.

"If you cooperate, the Piutes will come and find them alive. You wouldn't like to see them hurt, would you? I didn't think so. . . .One of them says she knows you. Her name is Della."

Roark said nothing, but his eyes narrowed.

"You see?" Thomas said with a smile. "I can always trust a Christian to do what's right. I knew Samuel would come. And I know you're not going to force me to shoot you in the back. So let's not waste anymore time. I've no intention of getting caught here and loosing my scalp."

"For Shaun's sake, spare Samuel. Get him out of here."

"I won't have him back in Virginia City hounding me. After this, he may even turn me in, who knows?"

"What about Jade?"

Thomas scanned him. "You're real interested in my daughter. Don't tell me you're—"

"She's ill. She might have died this winter."

Thomas grew sober. The green eyes mellowed slightly, then went blank. "I know. . .she always has been weak. That claim on Seven-Mile has rich ore. I'm going to hit a real bonanza, Montgomery. When I do, Jade will be well taken care of. I'll send the three of them back East."

"If you don't gamble it all away."

"Shut up."

"You'll also have a little trouble convincing the younger Ramos. By having his two brothers shot, you've riled a rattler. He's a worse hothead than the others. I'd say he won't rest until you're dead."

158

"Samuel has the paper showing I own the claim. It's legal enough."

"Bill Stewert doesn't think so."

"Bill Stewert will change his mind when he gets a percentage of the mine."

"You don't know Stewert."

"As for the Ramos brothers, I didn't kill them. The younger boy will understand that."

"Maybe you weren't on the roof that night, but the men there were following your orders. You also shot at me when I was at Seven-Mile. You almost killed Jade; she was there."

"I didn't see Jade at Seven-Mile. It was Jesse and Ernie who were on the roof with Letterman. They're waiting for me now—so they think. I have a feeling the Piutes will find them first."

"I don't know what's worse, Thomas, drawing on a man face to face, or standing back and allowing others to do your killing for you. If you let the Piutes raid Williams' Station without warning them, you're guilty of murder."

"Is it my fault if two stupid brothers manhandled a couple of squaws and got the Piute braves up in arms? I had nothing to do with that. It just worked out this way. I can't say I'm sorry. Too much is at stake for me to be generous. For once in my life, I'm going to get lucky."

"You've cheated and killed to get your hands on a claim that isn't yours. I wouldn't call that luck."

"You can preach to those two squaws. Get up there, Montgomery. Move."

Roark ducked his head to enter the cave. But couldn't tell how far back it went into the hill. Thomas kept his distance, as if expecting Roark to turn suddenly and attack. Ahead, Roark saw two women huddled in a darkened corner with a glowing lantern above their heads. One was very young and glared daggers at him. The other let out a gasp. "Mr. Montgomery!" Della cried.

"Far enough, Montgomery," said Thomas. "This is the end of your road."

Roark felt a sharp blow to the back of his head and he reeled. Consciousness ebbed, and a spinning hot darkness swept him into silence.

The Piutes came with a strange eerie yelp that sent the blood running cold in those who heard it.

Inside the Station, the Williams brothers knocked over their chairs trying to get to their feet. A dog barked frantically, and a woman screamed. An Indian swinging his tomahawk came galloping toward a man running for his horse. The Piutes charged, yapping like coyotes. Swiftly, the wooden structure was circled. Arrows flew. Within minutes, the station was blazing. The screams of the dying punctuated the devastation.

Not far away, Jesse and Ernie made a desperate charge toward the Carson River. Several braves chased after them. One Indian fell from Jesse's bullet, then two Piutes slowed down and drew their bows. The arrows, dipped in rattlesnake poison, found their mark with deadly accuracy. Jesse slipped from his saddle and splashed into the river. Ernie slowed to look back. "H-hey—Jesse! N-no—" His voice halted as the arrows struck him, and he, too, fell.

The Piutes rounded up the two horses, and one brave removed his scalping knife.

There was no sound in the cave but falling gravel, as

160

Roark raised himself to an elbow, his skull throbbing. He could hear movement outside the cave, and he squinted toward the shaft of sunlight to see the shadow of a woman near the entrance. She bent low and came toward him.

"Water, Mr. Montgomery?"

Della knelt before him and handed him a pitcher.

"Mr. O'Neil escaped," she said. "The others are all dead. Preacher Samuel is injured. There was rattlesnake poison on the arrow."

"He's alive?"

Yes, but unconscious. I think I got most of the poison out, but I can't tell yet."

Roark got to his feet, swaying a little as dizziness struck him. It dawned on him suddenly that the other Indian girl was gone and that he was not injured.

"What happened?"

"I told them who you and Samuel were. By then Samuel had been struck, but they left him alone after that. They understood he was a man of God, and that you had nothing to do with the men who ran this Station. They let you live."

"The girl?"

"She's gone back with them. I told them I would nurse Samuel first. There will be war now, Mr. Montgomery. The Pony Express went through here and saw what happened. By now, all Washoe is up in arms. They will come against my people."

Roark felt for his holster. Della removed it from where it hung across a rock and handed it to him.

"My apology for what happened here earlier. You're not hurt?"

"They did not hurt me. It is fitting that the Lord had

161

me here at this moment. You must tell Miss Jade that I have done what she said. I accepted the mighty Christ as my Saviour from sin. He is my Lord, now, and I was used by Him to spare you and Samuel. Jade must know her words to me and my father were not lost."

"I'll tell her. She'll be as pleased as I am. Can you take me to Samuel?"

"He's resting under a tree. He was too heavy for me to move."

He followed her from the cave into the sunshine, squinting as the light hurt his eyes. His head throbbed painfully.

"Are you sure Thomas O'Neil escaped?"

"He left a good while before the attack. I grieve for Miss Jade, her sister, and Shaun. Their father is worse than Garth. Garth drank too much, and he sinned against God. But he would never hurt anyone deliberately the way Mr. O'Neil has. He left you all to die. He is hard to understand. He had such a nice smile."

Della led the way across the hill. "I trusted him at first because he looked like Miss Jade. But his heart is far from being like hers."

Roark took in the charred structure that was once Williams' Station. The smell of smoke hung in the air, and he saw the wind pick up a man's hat and send it tumbling through the dust.

"How many need to be buried?"

"I found five. . . .I couldn't stop the raiding party from taking your horses, but they left me a mustang to ride back. You can take him. Samuel will need to ride. The Lord has helped me so far. He will continue to do so. You had better go. If the braves come back, they will not let you and Samuel go again."

"Why not come back with us? Jade would be happy to have you."

Della shook her head. "I teach my mother's brother of the true God. I tell them that Pah-Ah is not God. He can do nothing for them. But the mighty Christ can do everything good."

"Remind me to have Samuel give you his Bible. You read?"

"Very much so."

"Jade will be pleased that you've become a missionary among the Indians. It was something she wanted to do, but the Lord has called you."

Della smiled for the first time. "I am her spiritual child. Do you think Samuel will give me his Bible?"

"He will. Samuel?" he called out.

"Here, lad!"

Samuel had propped himself up against the back of a tree; his face brightened when he saw Roark was not hurt.

"Got an arrow in me, lad, but Della's patched me up."

Roark wasted no time. He checked the wound and saw that she had done the best job possible.

"Della told me what happened," Samuel said. "Sorry, lad. It was my fault for getting you into this. I should have known better." His voice grew husky. "I keep hoping Tommy will change."

Roark took a pitcher of water from Della and handed it to him. "We're still alive," he said with a smile. "What else do we have to complain about? But we won't be if we don't get out of here."

"This is bad stuff that's happened, lad. Many more

will die before it's over. Virginia town's full of hotheads. They'll be screaming for vengeance before they even know the reason behind the raid."

"I doubt if the reason would matter. Instead of negotiating with Winnemucca, who probably doesn't even know what his bucks did, they'll turn against the entire Piute nation."

"The Piutes are already meeting to form a war party," said Della. "There was talk of an ambush against the company from Virginia City. They will lure them into the desert near the mouth of the Truckee. There is a narrow, rocky defile there that leads to a valley."

"I know of the place," said Samuel. "It's close to the shores of Pyramid Lake. It's the right place for an ambush, if that's what they're planning."

"Can you ride?" Roark asked him.

"Just get me on the saddle."

When Samuel was astride the mustang, Roark looked at Della. "I don't feel comfortable leaving you on foot like this."

"I've been in worse situations, Mr. Montgomery. I have a feeling that a friend will be waiting for me on the way."

"A friend?"

She smiled. "A buck. . .I think he's watching us now. You better go."

Roark's eyes scanned the hills but saw nothing, and he didn't expect to. Piutes were too smart for that.

"Let us part with a prayer," said Samuel.

Obediently she bowed her dark head and listened as Samuel committed her to the safe keeping of Christ.

When he had finished, Roark turned to Samuel and

held out his hand. "Your Bible."

Samuel's face registered surprise at the request, then he glanced down at Della. Her dark eyes shone, and her black hair whipped in the wind. He smiled and reached into his old frock coat to produce the small black book.

"To Della," said Samuel O'Neil, as he handed it to her. "May you use it wisely, lead many to our precious Saviour, and be the godly mother of ten braves who serve the Lord."

She smiled, and took the Bible. "Tell Miss Jade she has written her name on my heart."

"I will," said Roark softly, and watched her run ahead and disappear.

"Whew," said Samuel, glancing again at the brown hills and wiping his brow with a handkerchief. "I'm a man of faith, lad, but I don't believe in tempting folly. Let's get out of here—fast."

Chapter 14

The front door of the cabin flew open and Shaun burst in. "Jade! Pa—Pa's here!" he stammered, eyes wide. "Our Pa is home!"

She sucked in her breath. "Here? Pa?"

"He's in Uncle Samuel's dugout! Come on!"

Jade went weak, then rallied. Thomas O'Neil was in Virginia City! Impossible! Or was it? A terrible suspicion gripped her heart. Had the message been a trap set for Roark?

Dear God. . .please, don't let it be true. . . .

Jade got up from the bed and rushed out the front door. Shaun had already run ahead of her.

Thomas O'Neil was on his haunches sorting through Samuel's papers when Shaun ran in. Jade followed and seeing him, paused.

"Pa! I brought her," he said excitedly. "Pa? Here's Jade."

166

Thomas tossed some papers and books aside, too engrossed in what he was doing to answer. Shaun stared at him with shining eyes, waiting.

Jade stood there. An endless moment passed before she could form the words. Surprisingly, they sounded calm.

"Hello, Father."

Thomas stopped when he heard her voice and turned, a book in his hand. Seeing her, his lashes blinked nervously, then a slight smile formed on his mouth. He stood slowly, staring at her, and set the book aside.

"Jade?"

She swallowed and nodded.

"Well, I'll be!"

How he had changed! She stared back. Thinner, sadder looking, much sadder. And there were lines etched in his forehead and cheeks. But the eyes were the same, like hers they glinted green. A smile flashed, bringing back memories of St. Louis. She remembered a Christmas tree one cold night long ago. . .her mother, Holly, Shaun as a baby. . . .

"Father!" She was in his arms. He held her, his face buried in her hair. His shoulders were shaking.

Jade wept. She didn't know how many minutes passed before she felt Shaun's hand tugging impatiently at her skirt.

"It's my turn," he kept saying quietly, but tensely. "It's my turn, Jade."

She pulled away and gave Shaun to Thomas. He knelt and hugged him, and the boy clung with his arms around his neck.

Jade heard him murmur, "What am I going to do. . . what am I going to do. . . ?"

167

Nervously, she pressed him, "Did you meet with Mr. Montgomery and Samuel at Williams' Station? Word came of a Piute raid—"

"It was a smoking ruin when I got there," Thomas interrupted tonelessly. "The Piutes killed everyone. We best not think of it now."

Jade felt faint. Was he telling the truth? She looked at him with horror, searching his expression, and saw tiny drops of moisture on his forehead. He tore his eyes from hers and mumbled, wiping his mouth on the back of his hand, "There's something I've got to do."

"Pa! Wait—" But Thomas pushed past her, almost knocking over the barrel chair. Jade hurried to the door after him, but he was already on his horse and riding down the slope toward town. She watched the direction he was going: The Delta Saloon.

"Where did he go?" cried Shaun. "He just got here."

Jade didn't turn at Shaun's disappointment. She was still staring toward town.

"He had to go away for awhile," she said dully.

"Again?" he cried.

She turned sharply at the bewilderment in his voice. His face was filled with pain. "Oh Shaun—" She tried to hold him, but Shaun jerked away, beginning to shake. His mouth clamped together, and his face turned pale. He whirled and ran away.

"Shaun! Come back, Shaun!"

She ran after him, but he was too fast for her. She saw him disappear in the shadows further up the hill. Understanding his need to be alone, she stood there feeling the wind tugging against her, fighting back the bitter tears. "Lord, only you can heal his hurts, only you know how deep they are."

Dark came and Thomas O'Neil had not returned. Shaun came quietly into the cabin, refusing to look at her. He tried to steal past, but she reached out and caught his arm. "Shaun?"

He smiled weakly. "It's okay. I'm okay now, Jade."

She held him tightly for a moment, then said softly, "Keeper's been looking for you. I think he's hungry. Why don't you feed him something? He needs you, you know. So do I, Shaun."

He nodded, but said nothing as he went into the next room. A few minutes later he came back holding Keeper in his arms. The dark eyes were quiet.

"Uncle Samuel said I can stay with him until I grow up." Then he changed the subject abruptly. "Pa's down at the Delta Saloon gambling."

Jade changed the subject, too. "I made some cornbread and bacon. It's still warm. Hungry?"

"I don't know. . .maybe. When's Samuel and Roark coming back?"

Jade's anxiety increased, but she held it in. "Maybe tomorrow. Sit down. I'll get your supper." She set the plate before him. "I'm going into town for Holly. She doesn't know Pa's here. I won't be long."

Jade entered the hotel and found Holly. When she heard Jade whisper that Thomas O'Neil was in town, her eyes widened and she stifled a gasp. "Where?"

"The Delta. Holly, there's something wrong. He said he didn't see them. And when I asked him about the raid on Williams' Station, he said it was over before he arrived."

"You don't think there was gun play do you?" Holly whispered.

169

"I think there was. I don't like the way he acts—or looks. I think that's why he went to the Delta."

"You mean to drink?"

"And to gamble. He uses them both as crutches. But I'm more worried about Samuel and Roark. If they were caught at Williams', we won't know for days. Oh Holly! I can't bear to think about them both being—"

"Don't say it, Jade; we don't know. Oh, I wish Dave were here."

"Why would Pa come back to Virginia City bold as day if he didn't think his trouble with Roark was over?"

"Unless he doesn't expect him to come?"

They stared at each other, each thinking the same thing.

"Oh, Jade. You don't think Pa would do such a thing?"

Jade spoke bluntly but in a whisper. "Kill Roark? And his brother Samuel?"

"Jade, are you asking me? I don't know! I saw Pa less when we were children than you did." Holly winced. "Oh, Jade, this is the worst moment in my life!"

Jade's fingers gripped her flesh. "Holly, if he did—if—"

"I can't handle it, Jade," she choked, trembling. "Don't even say it now. Let's wait. Maybe Samuel and Roark will ride into town tomorrow."

But early the next morning, the town was rocking with a different kind of news. One of the men who had ridden off with Henry Meredith's group returned, wounded.

"We were ambushed near Pyramid Lake. We rode into a valley, and suddenly, the heights above us on all

170

sides were filled with Piutes. We were outnumbered. Most of the boys were afraid and, in a panic, ran in all directions. Henry Meredith and Captain Ormsby made a heroic stand until everyone near them escaped. They were both killed, but their stand let the rest of us escape."

Virginia City was furious—and frightened. "Only a hundred men can be armed!" cried someone.

"Then send another wire to Governor Downey in California! We're trapped. We've got to have more men and more arms!"

Two anxious hours later, the return wire arrived from California. *Men and ammunition from the National Guard in Downieville being sent at once.*

As Jade stepped outside the hotel, she realized that she hadn't seen her father anywhere in town. Could he have gone out to Seven-Mile?

Shaun was at the other end of B Street. He cupped his mouth and called, "Jade!"

Jade waited as he came running down the boardwalk, his eyes shining with happiness. "They're back, Jade! Uncle Samuel and Roark! They rode in awhile ago; I've been looking for you."

Jade nearly broke down and wept. The Lord had been gracious! They were alive! Thomas hadn't killed them! *Oh, thank you, Lord!*

"Samuel's been wounded, but he's all right. Holly put him to bed."

"Wounded!"

"By a Piute! They were at Williams' Station when the attack took place! I can't wait 'til Uncle Samuel tells us all about it!"

When Jade and Shaun reached Samuel, Holly had him in bed, and he was drinking hot broth. She rushed over and knelt beside him. "Samuel! Thank God you're all right!"

His strong arm hugged her shoulder. "Takes more than an arrow to do me in."

"Where's Roark?"

"He rode out to Seven-Mile."

Jade was shaking. "I've got to find him."

"You just stay put, lass. Between Kidd Ramos and the Indians, I don't want you galavanting around. When Roark wants to find you again, he will. Just wait."

Jade motioned for Holly to divert Shaun. A minute later, when she was alone with Samuel, Jade said tensely, "Thomas is here."

His eyes were troubled. "I know. He's still got plans to claim the Ramos mine."

"We've got to stop him! Kidd Ramos won't back off."

"Neither will Tommy. I think he's gone a little beserk. There's going to be trouble neither of us can stop."

"But Roark can't stop both of them!"

"He can handle himself. He knows what he's doing." Samuel hesitated, then said, "Jade, the next few days will be some of the most difficult in your life. You've got to lean hard on the Lord, no matter what happens. Tommy won't listen to sensible truth, and I don't see him changing. If anything, he's gotten worse, and we've got to understand that."

"You saw him then? You talked to him?" Her voice held surprise. "Pa said he hadn't seen you or Roark."

"We saw him all right," he said dryly. "He was waiting

172

for us at Williams' Station with two gunslingers from Salt Lake."

"Then it's true. Pa did set an ambush? Oh Samuel, no!"

"It was a trap, just like Montgomery thought. I should have known. I almost got us both killed. Well, I've learned a good lesson."

"What happened? I thought it was the Piutes who attacked the Station?"

"It was, but it fit well into Tommy's plans. He didn't need to do anything but leave us there and hope the Indians scalped us both."

Jade turned her head. The idea that her father could do such a thing left her sickened.

"He's a hard man, Thomas. He's gone from drinking and gambling to hanging around with real killers. Little by little, his rejection of Christ has seared his conscience."

Samuel told her the rest of the story, and it was some time before Jade could control her emotions.

"You said Della was there? Was she hurt?"

"Ah, now we come to a bright spot! No, she's fine. We have blessings to thank our Lord for, too. He sends us sunshine along with clouds."

"She's truly accepted Christ?"

"Indeed. And you can rejoice for being the one that God used to bring it to pass. You came to Washoe to convert Indians, and through Della the seeds you planted will grow into a harvest. She said for me to tell you that you had written your name in her heart."

Jade leaned over and planted a light kiss on Samuel's forehead. "God is, indeed, good. Shaun wants to stay with you while I seek medical treatment in San Francisco."

Samuel's eyes twinkled. "I wasn't about to let him slip through my fingers. Don't you think I'm wise enough to see a future preacher?"

"Then it's settled? No matter what happens?"

"No matter what happens."

"You get some sleep now," she whispered.

"Get me Shaun first. He and I need to do some more talking."

The sun was setting behind Sun Mountain as Shaun left with Samuel. In the cabin alone, Jade paced, hearing the wind blowing about the window. Holly had gone to meet Dave Wylet who had ridden in from Carson as soon as he learned of the Piute raid.

Jade had spent much of the afternoon praying and trying to concentrate on the Scriptures, but Roark was always on her mind. Suppose he had to face both Thomas and Kidd Ramos—alone?

Feeling restless, Jade stepped out into the windy night. Below, the lights of Virginia City shone like hundreds of yellow stars.

He should come now, she thought, walking up the hill. It would be perfect. . . .She would run to him. He would embrace her. Thomas would have surrendered peacefully. . . .

Nothing moved on the slope but a gust of wind stirring the dust. She turned her face and held her breath until it passed. Vividly, she remembered the many times Roark had come to her aid. At this moment, when the night held the promise of danger, and perhaps great sorrow, she felt a tremendous longing for Roark. His strength and faith in Christ had fed her own. She must find him!

But where was he? In town? Had he ridden out to

174

the mine? She didn't dare saddle the mule and ride there alone with the Indian scare.

She saw old Toby climbing up the hill and walked over to meet him.

"Evening, Toby."

"Evenin', Miss Jade. How's Samuel?"

"Better. He's recovering from the poison. He should be much better tomorrow."

Toby tugged nervously at his beard and glanced back over his shoulder down the hill. "Seen your Pa today?"

Her tension mounted. "No. Not today. Not since last night. Why?"

"Montgomery's stayin' at the International. Saw him eatin' supper just awhile ago."

Her heart beat faster. "The hotel? Toby! You're sure?"

"It was him, all right. Looked to me like he had some serious business on his mind. Saw him loading his gun real careful like. Never seen a lawman look much calmer—"

Jade grasped her skirt and rushed past him.

Night had fallen across Virginia City. Roark Montgomery stepped out of the International Hotel feeling better now that he had bathed, changed into respectable clothing, and had something to eat. He wasn't cut out to be a miner, he decided. He preferred black broadcloth and white shirts to alkali dust, and a civilized place to eat dinner—preferably a terrace overlooking San Francisco Bay. Jade O'Neil, sitting across from him with those beautiful green eyes, would make the evening perfect.

He thought of her again. Then laughed at himself.

He couldn't get her off his mind. He had found himself attracted to her from the beginning, even when he hadn't wanted to be attracted. The young, innocent beauty, housing a pureness that reminded him of fine and delicate things, had been disturbing. And those eyes—they melted him with a look. Little did she know how they affected him.

Well, he couldn't think of that now. Regardless of what happened tonight, he was taking her to San Francisco. Her life depended on it. And his own? He put his hat on and automatically moved his jacket aside to test the ease of his belt and gun position. His eyes drifted down the street missing nothing. He had heard that Kidd Ramos was around looking for Thomas. He would need to stop him. Then, he must arrest Thomas O'Neil.

Arrest him! He was kidding himself, he knew. It was too simple and Roark knew it, but he kept avoiding the reality that he would need to use his gun. How could he be the man who killed Jade's father?

Roark stood on the street, thinking for a moment, feeling the wind in his hair. Down the street near the Delta Saloon a brawl had broken out. Not even the threat of the Piutes had sobered some of them.

Then he saw Jade running toward him down the walk. Roark muttered something under his breath and stopped. The timing couldn't be worse! She must not be there to see him draw against Thomas!

Jade paused when she saw the set of his jaw. She drew in a breath and walked slowly toward him.

"What are you doing here?" he breathed.

She managed to stay unruffled. She smiled and met his eyes steadily. "I was tired of waiting for you to show up. Do you know how worried I've been about you? First, the news about Williams' Station, and now my father and Kidd Ramos. Roark, I—"

"I'm sorry to have to put you through this, Jade. But we can't talk now. What I want to say to you must wait."

Jade noticed that he kept glancing down the street toward the Delta Saloon. He looked calm, almost careless, but she sensed that he was alert.

She knew what he had to do, and she was trembling, her hands cold. "Roark, you can't face two men—"

"Wait in my room." he interrupted quietly.

"What?" she breathed.

He smiled slightly. "My room. You'll be comfortable there."

The thought of a hotel room seemed like balm to her senses. She glanced back over her shoulder at the Delta but felt his hand on her arm, strong and steady.

"Besides, you look tired."

The suggestion that she appeared worn caused a drop in her spirits. Yet, he was right again. He seemed to know her so well. She was extremely tired. The last few days had been trying.

Roark, with another glance down the street that missed nothing, walked her into the International Hotel.

"Won't—people talk?"

"Fear not, fair damsel. Your reputation is perfectly safe. Besides," he said with a smile, "if I lock you in, I won't need to worry about you showing up where you shouldn't for the next few hours." His eyes glinted mischievously.

"Roark! You wouldn't dare!"

"Honey, I can't wait to begin taking you up on your dares."

Somehow Jade found herself standing in the open doorway of the hotel room, staring into a finely carpeted room, a plate-glass mirror and rich crockery, all hauled over the Sierras in mule-drawn freighters. It was enough to take her breath away.

"Like it?"

Her eyes met his in the mirror and saw them teasing her, but his voice was serious.

"Sometimes I think you're a tempter."

"Because I want to do something nice for you?"

What could she say to that? Her eyes went to the bed. Goose down! *What a night's sleep I'd have!* But she turned. "I can't, Roark. I must help care for Samuel."

"Don't you know better than to fib."

"I wasn't fibbing—"

He lifted her chin, and their eyes locked. "Yes, you were. Notice I was polite enough to say *fib*."

She tried to ignore his smile and the funny feeling his nearness brought. He was casually blocking the doorway by leaning there. They stared at each other for a long moment.

"By the way, your presence is requested at Montgomery House in San Francisco. I think you'll like it."

Montgomery House! She swallowed. Was his family that wealthy? Requested? What was he saying?

"You'll fit in well," he said smoothly. "My father will compliment my good taste. The place has been without a lady since my mother died."

Jade felt her heart slow, then pound. The suggestion was growing more obvious.

"I want to buy you a green satin dress with a bonnet to match, and one of those preposterous feathers peeping out the way I first saw you at Strawberry. I can't wait to see you looking like a princess. And when my father opens up that sanitarium in Arizona, we'll go there and stay until you're strong again. You can paint and sketch all you want. There might even be an Indian or two," he teased, "but let's make sure he's the friendly sort."

"Roark—? What are you saying?"

"Honey, you know what I'm saying." He leaned back and glanced down the hall. "I just don't have time to say it all—the way I want to."

Jade felt as if she would melt under his gaze.

Roark stood looking at her. Then he said slowly, "I'll say it now—even though this is a terrible moment. I intend to marry you. That is, I'm asking you to marry me. Jade, you must know by now how much I love you. I can't concentrate on much else. And that's a rather dangerous situation for me to be in, especially tonight."

A delighted gasp died in her throat. She stood there, dazed, holding back the mad desire to rush into his arms. Her eyes swept the formidable figure in black broadcloth, handsome, poised, and confident in the Lord. She almost laughed at the gift dropped into her lap from heaven. She had thought the Lord had forgotten her, and that she was unworthy of Beau—

Beau! Suddenly, she realized with crystal clarity that she had never loved him. Not like this, not the way she felt about Roark. She was exhilarated; she wanted to grab him and tell him how he lit a thousand flames within her heart.

But she simply stood there. "Oh!"

"Is that all? Oh."

She caught her breath, unable to speak. Her heart sprouted wings and for a moment she thought they would bear her away with giddy delight. Roark Montgomery was in love with her!

He folded his arms and smirked a little. "Well, I can see we're going to be very casual about this. This is a great night, Jade. I'm in the middle of stopping a gunfight, arresting your father, and asking you to marry me. It's all coming together very nicely, isn't it? After all, it's not every night I ask a beautiful woman to marry me, and then check to make sure my gun still comes out of the holster like silk." He tested it wryly. "Works fine." Again he glanced down the hall. "You don't suppose you could ease my frustration just a little and say 'yes' or 'I'll think about it,' or even 'no'?"

"I don't think this is a bit funny," she gasped finally.

"I don't either."

"I've always dreamed of being proposed to in moonlight, with blossoms, and nothing to disturb the enchantment."

"Just say yes, honey, and I'll made it up to you later."

"Yes! Oh yes!"

He stepped into the room. "Let Virginia City wait a minute."

In a moment he had swept her into his embrace. Her ears roared with the thunder of her heart.

"I love you," he whispered, as his lips sought hers. She stiffened, turning her face away, moaning at the dilemma facing them.

"You shouldn't kiss me, Roark," she choked. "I'm not

well. You know that."

"Just say what I want to hear."

Her eyes came back to his. "I couldn't love anyone else the way I love you," she gasped, melting into his arms.

"Beau?" he murmured.

"I don't remember any man named Beau. Who was he, do you know?"

"The name's Montgomery. Roark Montgomery. I want it branded on your heart the way Jade O'Neil is branded on mine."

"That happened a long time ago. . .when you introduced yourself outside Berry's Flat—but you still mustn't kiss me. . ."

"I know." Then his lips touched hers.

She went weak at the warm, gentle passion. She clung to him as the only solid thing in an exhilarating new world.

"Beautiful," he whispered. "You are a king's daughter, all glorious within."

Jade's eyes were still closed, and she took in a breath of air to clear her head. Roark steadied her and backed toward the hallway. "I'll see you in the morning. I've got a lot more to say."

For a moment she stood still, thinking of his kiss.

"If you hear anything out there, pretend you don't. There's nothing you can do now. I just want you safe, Jade. Now that I've found you, I don't want to lose you."

He glanced down the hall.

Suddenly she knew what he was about to do. "Roark, don't you dare lock—"

She rushed to reach him before the door shut, but

she wasn't quick enough. She heard the key in the lock. Jade grasped the ornate knob.

"Roark Montgomery! Let me out of here!"

There was no answer. She heard his steps die away down the hall. Exasperated, and somehow frightened, she sank back helplessly against the door.

Chapter 15

As Roark walked down the street, he heard someone call his name. He stepped to the side, but it was only Dave Wylet.

"Heard there's trouble. Thought you might need help. Ramos was heard swearing vengeance over his brothers. Thomas O'Neil is here, boasting that he's struck a silver bonanza out at Seven-Mile. Ramos is on his way, aimin' to settle the claim once and for all."

"Boasting of a silver find will just anger Ramos more."

"That's what I figure, too. It's as if he's doing it deliberately. He must know he'll rile Ramos into coming after him. Why's he doin' this, knowing his three kids are in town?"

"Dave, I appreciate your offer to help, but stay here.

This is my problem."

"C'mon, Roark. We've been friends too long for that. There's two of 'em. Maybe more. I can't just stand by doing nothing. Swear me in!"

"No. Go back to Holly."

"I can't, Roark. I'm goin' to be there, just in case, whether you swear me in or not. So let's go."

The Delta Saloon was crowded. Eyes turned in their direction as they walked in. It seemed as if everyone expected something to happen. Wylet moved to the back of the room and seated himself with his rifle.

Thomas O'Neil was seated at a green-baize poker table. For a moment Roark watched him. Thomas was sober, but so absorbed with his gambling that he stared, transfixed, at the cards. His eyes were fever bright. The shuffle of the deck and the clink of chips had hypnotized him.

Roark walked up to the table. "Hello, Thomas."

He started, then stood up, a strangely cold and brittle look in his eyes as he recognized Roark. "I heard you were back. How's Samuel?"

"He'll make it."

Thomas flashed a smile. "Had no doubt he'd survive to preach another sermon."

"Ramos is coming, but I'm going to arrest you before he gets here."

"Sorry. . .I never did care much for 'Frisco. The fog, you know? Too damp.

"Get out of here, Montgomery. It's between me and Ramos. Take Jade and leave."

"Let's go, Thomas."

"You'll have to shoot me first. That will end everything between you and Jade. Besides—I can take you."

"I wouldn't try it."

"Fast, huh?"

"I wouldn't have opted to put a badge on if I wasn't. I'm not a fool."

Hard green eyes held his. "You're saying I am?"

"I've run into dozens of men like you, Thomas. Each one brags about how good he is. His worth as a man is wrapped up in what he can do with a gun. The others are like you, too—each one scared inside."

"Fine preaching, Montgomery. But I'm not afraid. I'm good, you know? Real good. Maybe the best there is. I can take you—" He turned to the room of men and said loudly, "and I can take Langford Peel, Sam Brown, Eldorado Johnny—"

"Like I said, you're all the same," Roark said calmly. "Scared of facing responsibility. You'd rather hide behind a gun than worry about a daughter dying of tuberculosis, or a little boy so lonely for his father he finds emotional comfort in a cat."

"Shut up!" Anger laced the words.

"My father was one of the finest surgeons in the country. Yet, I don't hate you for crippling his hand. There is a forgiveness that isn't human."

"I said shut up, Montgomery!" Thomas stepped back, feet apart.

At once the room divided and cleared. Those nearest the door slipped out. The dealer stood up from his chair and backed off.

Roark's hand was inches from his gun. "Don't make me do it, Thomas."

There was a ruckus near the door. "Murdering scum! You killed my brothers!"

Thomas glanced toward the door. Kidd Ramos, eyes blazing, held a Winchester aimed at O'Neil's heart.

185

"Stay out of this Ramos," warned Roark. "I'm taking O'Neil back to San Francisco. You've got your claim. Back off."

"Yeah? Why should I? No confession on his part will bring my brothers back!"

"Try to kill Thomas, and I'll be forced to add you to their number."

"I ain't staying out of it, Montgomery. You come between O'Neil and—"

Suddenly, Thomas drew and fired at Ramos, striking him in the chest. Ramos, thrown backward, nevertheless fired the Winchester. The bullets found their target, and Thomas crashed against the gambling table, the cards and chips falling with him, glass shattering.

Ramos staggered forward and fell.

Roark looked across the room at Wylet. Wylet simply stared back. No one else in the room saw the sigh of relief that slipped silently from Roark's lips.

Silence gripped them as they stepped outside into the night. The sky was clear and black, and the stars were shining. The wind ruffled their jackets. It was over.

"I'll tell the others," said Wylet.

"Have Samuel speak with Shaun. He'll do it right."

Wylet nodded, took off his hat, and ran his fingers through his hair. Then, he put his hat back on and walked up the street toward Sun Mountain.

Roark stood alone in the night. The saloon's piano music was playing again. He walked back to the International Hotel.

"Good evening, Mr. Montgomery," said the proprietor. "Pleasant weather we're having. A little cool for the month of June, however."

186

"I'd like another room for the night."

"Sir?"

"Miss O'Neil is asleep in my room."

"Oh, yes. . .I see, of course."

Roark paid for the room. "Have some coffee sent up, will you?"

"At once, Mr. Montgomery."

"When does the stage leave?"

"Nine o'clock on Friday. Do you wish to buy a ticket?"

"Yes. Make it two."

In the room, Roark sank into a chair. The wind moved the curtain at the open window, and the distant sound of music floated up. He let his mind wander. With God's help, his father would know how to treat Jade. Shaun could come and visit anytime he wanted, and he would work with Samuel to see that the boy had good schooling. Dave Wylet would see to Holly.

He got up and walked to the open window, moving the curtain to look down on the town. He could let Virginia City take care of the Piutes, and its ore mining, running stamp mills, and fighting over claims. Let them have their silver—even if his percentage in the Solomon mine was about to pay off handsomely—but it was time for him to go home to San Francisco. His mouth curved. Who would have thought that when he arrived at Berry's Flat a few months ago he would be returning to Montgomery House with a bride? He smiled as he anticipated his father's reaction when the coach brought Mr. and Mrs. Roark Montgomery up the drive.

He drank a cup of coffee, then decided that Jade probably wasn't asleep either. Setting the cup down, he said aloud, "What's the matter with me? Why don't I just go see her the way I want to?"

Jade heard the key in the lock and turned from the window, hands on hips, green eyes sparkling. Roark stopped in the doorway and leaned his shoulder against the doorframe. She rushed toward him, ready with words, but the words died unspoken. By his expression she knew, and she paused.

They looked at each other for a long moment, then she said, "It's over, Roark?"

"It's over, honey."

She swallowed, afraid to ask. "You?"

He sighed and lifted both hands. "No. Ramos. They're both gone."

She came into his arms, and he held her, comforting her while she wept for the stranger who had been her father.

"Everything's going to be all right," he whispered, caressing her hair. "It's time you and I left Virginia City. We can have Samuel marry us tomorrow and leave Friday morning on the stage. Would you like that? We can have Shaun and Holly at our wedding."

She looked up at him. "Oh, Roark, it would mean so much to share our wedding with them." She paused, then asked hesitantly, "You're sure your father won't mind an O'Neil for a daughter-in-law?"

"One glimpse of those green eyes and he'll fall head over heels in love. I think you'll love him, too. He's a special kind of man, Jade. One God has used mightily, and one He will still use. In Arizona, you'll have the best opportunity of getting well."

Her eyes searched his. "Do you think so, Roark? Will it turn out well? Our life—our marriage?"

188

He smiled. "When two people are committed to the Lord and to each other as we are? We have everything working for us."

She smiled up at him. "I think I'm going to love you too much."

"You can never love me too much," he whispered huskily.

She rested her cheek against his chest.

"Roark?" her voice was quiet, "suppose I don't get well?"

"Whatever happens, Jade, I will never love you less. We're going to be happy, you and I. We're going to live each day to the fullest."

"And leave our future to God," she added brightly. "He knows the beginning from the end. I read some wonderful verses tonight while you were away. I was praying about everything, then about you and me. It's Jeremiah 29:11 through 13. I wanted to share them with you."

He released her, and she crossed the room to where his Bible rested on the table. She opened it, then looked up at him and smiled. She read softly, "For I know the thoughts that I think toward you, saith the Lord, thoughts of peace and not of evil, to give you an expected end. Then shall ye call upon me, and ye shall go and pray unto me, and I will hearken unto you. And ye shall seek me, and find me, when ye shall search for me with all your heart."

Her eyes met his, unknowingly brightened by a glow on her cheeks, and a glimmer of new light in her eyes.

Roark slipped his arm around her and read the verses she was showing him. "I underlined them," she said.

He planted a kiss on her forehead, then on her lips.

"Our life passage, Jade. We'll face our tomorrows with confidence and joy—as we seek Him with all of our hearts."